Wolf Pact

Melissa de la Cruz

Wolf Pact

Melissa de la Cruz

Story by Melissa de la Cruz and
Michael Johnston

www.atombooks.net

ATOM

First published in the United States as four ebooks in 2012 by Hyperion
First published in Great Britain in 2012 by Atom

Copyright © 2012 by Melissa de la Cruz

The moral right of the author has been asserted.

A CIP catalogue record for this book
is available from the British Library.

ISBN 978-1-907410-18-5

Typeset in Baskerville by M Rules
Printed and bound in Great Britain by
Clays Ltd, St Ives plc

Papers used by Atom are from well-managed forests
and other responsible sources.

MIX
Paper from
responsible sources
FSC® C104740

Atom
An imprint of
Little, Brown Book Group
100 Victoria Embankment
London EC4Y 0DY

An Hachette UK Company
www.hachette.co.uk

www.atombooks.net

PART ONE

Sometimes it's necessary to go a long distance out of the
way in order to come back a short distance correctly.

Edward Albee

Breakout

His earliest memory was of the collar around his neck. Itchy, heavy, tight. From the beginning he wanted it off. It reminded him every day that he was born a slave.

He was a wolf, a beast of hell, a captive, but for now his will and his mind were his own. He had family to protect, brothers and sisters from his den who shared his fate. Taken from their mothers at birth, the pups bonded together and as they grew, he led them to think the unthinkable, that one day, they might break free of their chains.

Freedom was a faraway dream, though. The future was far more likely to hold horrors he couldn't even imagine. Every wolf was turned into a hellhound on their eighteenth moon day, as young wolves turned too early ran the risk of death. So the masters waited until they were strong enough for the change. When he turned eighteen, his life would be over. He would lose his identity, his soul. His every thought and action would be controlled by Romulus, the Hound of Hounds, the Great Beast of Hell.

One day during his sixteenth year, Master Corvinus pulled him aside. Corvinus was their battle sergeant, and like the rest of the masters, he was a former angel, banished from Paradise, a veteran of the War of Heaven. Corvinus was the one who exercised them in the pits, who monitored their progress, who put their names on the lists.

Corvinus had noticed his talent at a recent battle, how he had been able to dodge his adversary's blows with graceful precision—as if he knew where they would land before they did, as if he could see one or two or even three seconds ahead—and the fight had been over before the bell finished ringing.

His name was put on the top of the lists, and he made his way up through the tournaments, through the pits. He kept winning. Every round. He beat them all. Gorg the giant, so called because he was bigger than any of them; Odoff the giant-killer, because he was the first who bested Gorg; Varg; Tatius; Aelia, the vicious she-wolf with the long claws; Drusus; Evander. He had just had to win one more round for the top prize.

But to his shock, he was bested at the trials and not made alpha. After his defeat, he waited for them to come and take him away. He waited, but no one came. The masters seemed to have forgotten about him.

4

Not so. Instead of killing him, Corvinus brought him before the general.

Romulus was a massive creature, fearsome, with glinting crimson eyes and silver pupils; he was more than human yet not quite wolf, a startling combination of both, as all hellhounds were. Romulus studied him. "Regardless of your performance in the arena, they tell me you are the one. That once you've shed the wolf skin for hellhound form, you will be a mighty warrior, one of the strongest Hell has ever known. The Dark Prince himself has seen it. Lucifer has entreated me to make you my heir. We shall not wait until your eighteenth moon day to make you one of us."

Never, *he whispered to himself afterward.*

Never what? *Ahramin asked. She was the oldest wolf in their den, the fiercest of the she-wolves. Beautiful, dangerous.*

I'm never going to be a hound. I'll die before they turn me.

And how are you going to do that? *She motioned to the collar he wore, the one all the wolves wore.* That collar will keep you from self-destructing. The masters don't like to waste a good dog.

Once they were hellhounds they would assume their true form, they would walk upright, they would speak the language of the masters. They would carry black swords and wear armor. They were the dogs of war, Hell's army, and Lucifer, it was said, was preparing a grand campaign.

That was his fate; that was the fate of all wolves.

But there had to be a way out. Since his defeat, he had not been lazy. He spent his time watching the hounds. There's a sword, *he told her.* I saw it. An archangel's sword. The hounds stole it, but it's here, they keep it at the armory. It can break our collars. We can escape. We can leave this place.

Ahramin looked skeptical.

Trust me.

He spent the next week formulating a plan. Their collars hindered their power and tethered the wolves to the underworld. He was certain that once they were broken and the wolves were free, they could easily subdue the trolls who guarded them, but once they were out of the den, how would they get aboveground? How would they cross Hell's Gates into the land of the living? There were rumors that the Gates were falling, that the archangels' strength had been sapped—but the masters kept them in the dark, and there was no way to know what was true.

The great wolves of old used portals; that much he knew. The Praetorian Guard moved through passages, roads of space and time that allowed them to be anywhere and anytime in history. But the knowledge of the ancient wolves had been lost for centuries. The passages were closed to him and his kind.

But Marrok believed they would open for him. Marrok told him to try. The white wolf was from the den across the river, and his greatest friend. Marrok knew about the chronologs, about the

6

passages, about their long and storied history. Marrok knew about his talent and told him to go, and the rest of them would follow. He hoped Marrok was right.

He waited until a night when the trolls seemed tired, when their guard was down, when the masters were distracted with other tasks, and he gathered the wolves of his den together.

I'm going tonight, *he said, looking at their eager young faces.* Who's with me?

The wolves looked to Ahramin. She had some misgivings, but ultimately she approved the plan, as he knew she would. She was as reluctant to be turned into a hound as any of them.

He'd stolen the sword earlier that day. It had been easy enough; it was a little thing, the size of a needle, and he'd kept it in his mouth. The locks on their collars broke at its touch. The freedom was almost debilitating; he could feel the power flood through his body, through his soul. Wolves were strong, stronger than the masters once, it was whispered—maybe it was true.

He led them past the trolls who guarded their dens, almost making it out the door when one of the younger wolves stumbled and twisted her ankle. Help! *she cried.*

She'll only slow us down, *Ahramin growled.* We'll come back for her.

No! Please! *Tala pleaded. Her big blue eyes locked on his, and he didn't see how he could refuse her.*

She's coming with us. *Tala had helped him when he was down; he owed her this much.*

This is a bad idea, *Ahramin warned.*

She was right.

Tala followed as they left the den, but her slower pace gave the hounds time to realize what was happening. They came, roaring and enraged, salivating at the thought of ripping the wolves apart, and they caught up to them right at the border between the worlds. The wolves were certain to be captured until Ahramin lunged for the master, ripping out his demon throat.

Go! *she yelled. Already the hounds were rounding up the others, locking collars on their necks, dragging them back down to the Ninth Circle of Hell.* I'll hold them here, go!

No! *cried Edon, who'd always loved her.*

You know I'm right, *Ahramin said. She was so brave, so fearless.* Do what you have to do.

More hounds were drawing closer.

In a moment, they would all be captured.

He closed his eyes and without thinking, only feeling, he opened a space between the worlds, breaking through the gate that kept them in the underworld. Before him opened a path, blazing with light and surrounded by fire. Follow me, *he called to the pack.* Quickly! *he yelled, pushing Tala forward.*

One by one they jumped over the ring of fire and into the light that stretched far off into the distance.

They fell out onto a forest floor, and the ring closed behind them. He was in agony, and beside him, he heard his brothers howl. Their limbs were stretching; they were losing their fur, torsos lengthened, their facial features receding.

"What's happening?" someone cried, and it was no longer the growl of a wolf but a higher-pitched almost melodic sound. A voice.

He looked down to see hands, bruised and bloodied and covered in calluses.

"I think . . . " he said cautiously, finding it strange to hear his thoughts spoken out loud for the first time, "I think we've become human."

ONE

The world was ending. The world was on fire. He had never seen anything so bright. So this was the sun. His eyes hurt from its brilliance. He was cold and hot all at once, shivering and sweating, and he realized he was naked. They all were. They were four boys on the side of the road, shuddering from the cold and broken from the heat.

How had they gotten here? He remembered running into the portal, landing in the woods, realizing they'd somehow shifted to human form. They'd been shocked and exhausted, and he wondered if they'd somehow wandered back and been transported somewhere else. It didn't matter now; they just had to figure out how to function in this new world, how to figure out if they'd been followed, if the hounds were on their tail. With their collars off, the hounds would be able to trail them only by their scent. They had some time, he hoped. Time to get used to this new world, time to run and hide, time to plan to free the others.

"Here." He looked up to see Tala standing over him. Unlike them, she was clothed, wearing some sort of black-and-red checked suit, in a material that looked warm. The clothes were huge on her; her small frame was drowning in them. She handed him a similar pair. "Pajamas," she said. "That's what they're called, for sleeping." She was speaking the human language, and he could understand her.

Tala placed a blanket on Mac's shoulders. Mac was the youngest of the brothers, unsure of himself and often scared. Tala seemed to have appointed herself his care-taker, and Lawson was grateful for it.

"There are more back there." She pointed to a small building on wheels not too far away.

He gathered Edon and Rafe with him, Tala, and Mac; the five of them were all that was left of the pack—such a small number—and they walked slowly toward the trailer. Tala had already broken the lock on the door. They rummaged through the drawers in the small beat-up compartment, which was even shabbier than the den they'd left behind. So this was what it was like above-ground, he thought. And here they were, stealing from folks who were no better off than they were.

The clothes were ill-fitting, but covered them. He looked in the mirror, shocked to see his human reflection. It was said among the wolves that Lucifer's curse was what had turned them into animals. Lawson saw that he had dark brown hair, brown eyes, a scrawny build. This was what he'd fought for, a new life, a new beginning, and he realized he wanted a new name to go with it. The old one wouldn't do anymore. Not in this new world. But what? He found a blue jacket on a nearby chair and put it on, grateful that it was warm.

"Lawson," Mac said, pointing to the white tag on his lapel. "Your name," Mac joked. "And mine is Malcolm."

Lawson. That would fit. He could live with that. It sounded brand-new to his ears, and he liked that.

"That's me," Lawson said. "From now on."

Mac nodded.

Lawson looked around at his brothers. Rafe was large and hulking; Mac, or Malcolm, as he wanted to be called now, was too skinny; Edon, out of all of them, looked almost normal, handsome with his bright golden hair, his features almost like those of the masters, except without their frightening scars.

"You look good," Lawson told him. "But the rest of us . . . " He grinned.

Edon didn't look at him, didn't smile, didn't answer.

They had left Ahramin behind, and Lawson wondered if Edon would ever forgive him for that. But he had no time to worry about that now; they had to figure out what they were going to do now that they were up here, now that they were free. His stomach rumbled, a low, almost gurgling sound, and he realized none of them had eaten in at least a day. "We have to find food," he said.

"There's a refrigerator in the kitchen," Tala said. She was slim and small, quiet-looking, almost plain, but her blue eyes were the same as before, kind and gentle.

"How do you know so much?" he asked her. She knew the words for everything. She knew how this place worked.

"Master Quintus would read to me sometimes, books from this world. I was his favorite pet." She shrugged.

They took only as much as they needed: a loaf of bread, a jar of something green, "pickled," Tala called it. He didn't want to take any more, to steal from those who had so little, but he didn't yet know how else they would manage. And they had to survive. So that someday they could go back and save the rest of the wolves. So that someday everyone would be free. Lawson thought of the portal he had left open for the others. Marrok would not come until he had Romulus's chronolog—he had been adamant that they could not leave the underworld without the device—and Lawson hoped his friend knew what he was doing.

After their first week aboveground, they learned. To sleep in the parks, which was easier than sleeping in the woods. To scavenge from garbage cans. To filch a wallet from a back pocket, or a purse from behind a chair in a coffee shop. To steal from those who seemed like they could afford it, shiny people in handsome clothes, three-piece suits and well-cut dresses.

They learned the name of the place they had landed: Hunting Valley, Ohio. And how to adjust to the sun, the noise, the nighttime cold, the daytime heat. And that aboveground was an awful lot like hell; the underworld was just a darker version of the world above it. He was disappointed by this; he'd hoped for more. Tala teased him, told him he was thinking of Paradise, and the wonders of Elysium were not meant for the likes of them. They were lucky enough to have crossed into this world; he didn't have to go and get ambitious all of a sudden.

Like Tala, Mac seemed to have a better sense of what they'd gotten themselves into. In Hell, he'd discovered the secret library the masters kept, and had taught himself to read the books describing things they didn't have down there: art, music, poetry. "There's beauty up here," he told them. "We just have to find it."

But Lawson didn't know if they would ever find it. They were barely making it day by day. That there was no sign of hellhounds gave him little comfort. If he and his wolves had been able to cross Hell's Gate, then it was reasonable to expect that the hounds would be able to do so as well. There was also the matter of Edon's stubborn refusal to talk. Edon was mute, broken, and Lawson was starting to get impatient. "We'll go back for her," he told his brother again and again. "We won't leave her behind."

But Edon's silence said it all: they already had.

Thank god he had Rafe to help him there—Rafe had been especially strong as a wolf, and as a human he was large, dense with muscle. He flexed his biceps often, preening. "Can't keep up a body like this without food," he'd say, and poke Edon in his stomach, or pinch his arm. Edon never said a word, but finally, he snatched a sandwich out of Rafe's hands one day, and ever since he had been scavenging with them.

"I knew I'd get him eventually," Rafe confided in Lawson. "He never could stand it when I teased him."

"Well, keep going," Lawson said. "He'll have to talk at some point."

"Give him time," Tala said. "He's been through so much."

"We all have," Lawson reminded her. "And there is still so much to do."

"Be gentle with him," Tala said, and her eyes showed her own sadness. Lawson had almost forgotten that she and Ahramin were sisters—not just in spirit, not just because they were from the same den, but because they were from the same mother—and that Tala was mourning as well. "She was tough, and she didn't have much time for someone weak like me, but I loved her. I miss her. I wish she was here with us."

"We all do," he said.

"He'll come around eventually," Tala said, putting a hand on his arm.

Lawson hoped so. He felt guilty enough leaving Ahramin behind as it was, and with every day Edon passed in silence, he felt worse. But he had to worry about the pack; he didn't have time to focus on individual concerns.

That afternoon he gathered them together to strategize. "We have to start thinking about the future. We can't keep living like this, stealing and scrounging and never sure where we're going to sleep."

There was silence, then a surprising response, from a scratchy, low voice that resembled a familiar growl. "We can't stay in any one place too long," Edon said. "We have to keep moving, before the hounds catch our scent. We don't know how long the Gates will hold them back."

"My thoughts exactly." Lawson nodded, relieved to have his brother speaking at last.

"We need to learn more about this world," Malcolm said, ever the sensible one. "I'm the only one who knows how to read. And none of us can write. We need to find a place that's safe for us. This isn't it." He waved his hand around the park they'd camped in, a bleak stretch of asphalt covered in dingy wooden benches where they'd eventually sleep.

"Where should we go?" Rafe asked, looking to Lawson for answers.

"Perhaps I can be of assistance," boomed a voice from behind them. How could Lawson have missed someone sitting on one of the park benches? He could have sworn no one was there. But sure enough, when he turned around, a man was sitting there, an older gentleman with about three-quarters of a smile on his face. He was small and round, dressed in fine clothes that had seen finer days—a brown corduroy jacket and neat slacks, but Lawson could tell they were old and worn, the collar was frayed, and the hems of his coat were thread-bare.

"You must be the wolves. Allow me to introduce myself," the man said. "I'm Arthur Beauchamp."

TWO

"I'm a warlock," he explained, in response to their alarmed looks. "Actually, I'm a Norse god, doomed to mid-world, but why complicate things? That's another story."[1]

"Is that how you know us? Is that how you recognized who—what—we are?" Lawson asked.

Arthur cocked his head to one side. He exuded a shabby geniality that was difficult to dislike. "Yes, and no, I suppose. Warlocks aren't allowed to use their powers. Those of us who choose to live in the open must pretend to be mortal. I've been in hiding for some time now, so I suppose I'm not . . . *strict* . . . about keeping a rein on my

1 You can find it in *Witches of the East*, available in paperback and e-book.

magical activities. But I've been looking for you for a very long time. A friend asked me to do her the favor of finding you. She said that one day I would come upon a pack of young wolves, and they would need my help."

"We need some kind of help all right," Edon muttered.

Lawson supposed it was a good thing that Edon was speaking, but why did he have to choose now, and with that tone?

"Well, that's what I'm here for," Arthur said, not at all perturbed. "Come, we have much to discuss, and you can't stay here."

Lawson looked around at the other wolves. It was easier to read their faces in their human forms. Malcolm was scared, Rafe was skeptical, and Edon was indifferent. It was Tala's face that made the decision for him: there was an openness to the possibility that Arthur really was there to help, that he could be trusted, and Lawson trusted that.

"Okay," he said.

Arthur packed all of them into his beat-up van, introduced them to fast-food takeout, then drove for several hours until they reached his apartment in the city. "This is an older part of Cleveland, a bit forgotten—like me," he said. It was a cramped one-bedroom with one bathroom, and he apologized for the size, but Lawson assured him they'd be fine—they were used to the tight quarters of the den, after all.

"I'd use magic to make it bigger, but that would be conspicuous," Arthur told them. "What small amount of magic I've used to increase the space is all for storage." He opened what appeared to be a closet door and turned on the light.

Lawson could barely see in, but apparently Malcolm had gotten an eyeful right away. "Whoa," he said, and then ran into the room with a whoop.

Arthur wasn't kidding about using magic, Lawson realized when he saw that the closet expanded on the inside to the size of a small library, with long mahogany tables and enormous bookshelves. "I thought this was more important than extra bedrooms," Arthur said. "We have much work to do, all of us."

"What kind of work?" Rafe asked suspiciously.

"As young Malcolm said, you need to learn to live in this world," Arthur replied. "And you need to learn about the world you came from. The wolves have a long history, and I'm not sure how much of it you know."

"We know some," Lawson admitted. The masters were reluctant to teach the wolves much about their past, but stories were handed down. They knew that wolves had lived in mid-world once and had served a special purpose. Lawson told Arthur what they knew about the Guard and the passages. "Does that sound right?" he asked.

The old man nodded. "You've got the basics down. But there's a lot more to the story than just what's happened to the wolves, and there's a lot more at stake now that the dark fallen—those 'masters' of yours—are making trouble. We Norsemen don't interfere with the lost children of the Almighty, it's part of our restriction. But you are not similarly bound by our covenant, which is possibly why I was asked to help you. Now let's all go into the library and get started. First things first, nothing happens without literacy."

It felt to Lawson as if they spent every moment of the next month in the library. They must have slept at some point, bodies piled on top of each other as when they'd been puppies in the den, but whenever they were awake, they were in the library, studying.

He was glad they picked it up quickly; even Arthur was surprised. "Now we'll have more time to spend on the more interesting things," the warlock said, and introduced them to history books, both those written from the human perspective and those containing the alternative "true" history of the world. "For those of us more enlightened," Arthur put it, but Lawson knew he meant for those who had a connection to the world of magic.

Lawson was fascinated by how much misinformation had made its way through the various dens where the wolves lived in the underworld, interspersed with the things that were true. He knew, for instance, that after the War of Heaven, the Fallen had been cursed to live in mid-world as vampires, made to drink human blood to survive, reincarnating every cycle, and that the wolves had a tangled history with them that led to Romulus's betrayal and the punishment of the wolves at Lucifer's hand. The vampires—Blue Bloods, led by the arch-angel Michael—were wealthy and untouchable, Arthur explained, and from what Lawson heard about them, he thought that he and his pack had probably stolen wallets and purses from several Blue Bloods that first week.

But the vampires had problems of their own; the Dark Prince had returned in a different form, one the Blue Bloods had not suspected, launching an attack on the covens in Rio and New York. Lucifer had been thwarted for now, but Michael had disappeared, and the Silver Bloods—known to the wolves as their masters—were still causing havoc in this world. The vampires were going into hiding, but the Next Great War was coming, whether they were prepared or not, Arthur warned, and the wolves had a part to play in it.

"What do you know about chronologs?" Lawson asked Arthur.

"The chronologs were destroyed during the Crisis in Rome, I believe," Arthur said. "Why do you ask?"

"Because Romulus found one," Lawson said. "He wears it around his neck. He doesn't yet know how to use it. We heard the masters saying they think it's broken."

Arthur looked grim. "This is dark news you bring, young wolf. If Romulus finds an entrance to the passages ..."

Lawson nodded, hoping more than ever that Marrok had been successful in his part of the operation.

The books couldn't teach them everything they needed to know, so television filled the gaps. They watched and learned how to dress like normal teenagers or close enough that no one would suspect they were anything else. At seventeen, Edon was the oldest; Tala and Lawson were both sixteen, Rafe fifteen, and Malcolm twelve, their ages corresponding to a human life cycle. They had to learn how to be independent one day; they couldn't live with Arthur forever, as hospitable as he was. Lawson knew Edon was right—it was safer if they moved every so often, to keep the hounds off their scent. Arthur couldn't keep them safe; he couldn't even use his magic without fear of reprisal from his betters.

Finally, it was time to move on. Lawson gathered them around, told them the plan. They were leaving the next day with Arthur's blessing; they had to keep moving, lest the hounds catch their scent.

"There's just one thing I want to do before then," Tala said to him. "Can you help me?" she asked with a shy smile, a smile that was starting to mesmerize him.

"Of course," Lawson said. He had grown to like her even more in the time they had stayed with the warlock. Tala was unfazed by their new surroundings. She was excited by everything: colors, music, the sight of a yellow butterfly on the green grass. Arthur had taught them the seasons, and it was currently spring. They had never heard of such a thing in the underworld. Lawson was glad she could find happiness. All Lawson saw when he looked around were shadows. The hellhounds would come for them, he was sure. It was just a matter of when. They had to prepare.

Tala whispered in his ear. "Meet me in the bathroom in fifteen minutes."

*

Lawson squeezed into the tiny space to see clumps of brown hair on the floor and Tala leaning over the sink. "What are you doing?" he asked, horrified. He hadn't realized how much he liked her long hair until he saw that she'd cut it all off. She was leaning over with her head under the faucet, and the water running off it was a violent purple.

"I'm dyeing it," she said. "I have to make sure to rinse it all off. Can you make sure it's off my neck?"

He did as she asked. He rinsed her hair, made sure that the water ran clear, that all the color was gone. When he touched her skin, he felt a shiver run through him. Pleasure, he thought.

She straightened up and wrapped a towel around her neck. "Thanks." Then he watched as she took a blow-dryer and teased her newly short hair into a spiky style. It was pink, he saw now, not that angry violet. It looked amazing.

"You can go now," she said. She caught his eye in the mirror. "But you don't have to." She was wearing a thin camisole that showed off her clavicles, and a pair of boxer shorts. It was not the first time he'd noticed her body—slim and boyish—the gentle curve of her chest, her small waist, but it was the first time he'd felt a sudden, intense desire to pull her toward him. The look she gave him was frank, confident, sure of his attraction, and it was making his face hot. She wanted him too; he could tell.

He stepped close to her, placed his hands firmly on her hips, and drew her toward him, a wolf with his mate. Their mouths were so close he felt her breath and wanted to feel her lips. Then came a sharp knock on the door.

"What are you doing in there?" Malcolm whined. "Some of us need to use the toilet."

Lawson coughed, his cheeks burning. "Hold on, I'm coming out."

"Me too," Tala said. She brushed his hands with hers. The implication and the disappointment were clear.

Next time.

THREE

*I*n the morning, they set out to find a new place to live, packing what few belongings they'd gotten from Arthur—secondhand clothes and books—into backpacks. They hitchhiked, moving east toward the coast, staying in a succession of small towns, never longer than a week in each. Lawson felt safer near the woods, so they shied away from the big cities. As the temperature rose, they spent summer on the rocky beaches of Maine, and when fall came, they began to move west. There was still no sign of the hounds, and in December they were back where they had begun, back in Hunting Valley, and they paid Arthur a short visit. The traveling had done them good. They passed for real humans and he was glad to see them looking well. They decided to stay in town, where he would be close by.

They found an abandoned house at the edge of the city, dilapidated and reeking of mildew but with several small bedrooms. It was located at the end of a broad cul-de-sac among several other houses that also seemed abandoned; despite the mildew it was in a newer development, the investors of which had apparently gone bankrupt before they'd even finished paving the streets. Many of the houses were half-built, slabs of concrete with pipes reaching upward, waiting for plumbing that would never be installed, for wood frames that would never be hammered into place. They planned to stay for a week at most, then move on, just as they had been.

Arthur had given them some money, so Tala took Malcolm to the store to buy groceries while the rest of the boys wandered off to look for jobs. Lawson got lucky right away. Since they'd been on their own, he'd learned the best way to find work was to hang around the parking lots of big-box stores where other unemployed men gathered, and quickly got himself hired as part of a ground crew. He spent the day clearing out someone's yard and was paid fifty bucks for his trouble.

A fortune to them.

He came home that night and handed Tala a small cardboard box. "For you."

"What is it?" she asked, opening the lid and looking inside.

"I saw someone order them. They looked good." He had watched, in front of the town bakery, as people pointed toward bread loaves and mouthwatering pastries, leaving the store with delicacies that smelled so delicious it almost drove him insane.

Tala picked up the pastry and bit into it.

"I think it's called a cream puff," he said.

She laughed at the joy of it. A tiny circle of cream dotted her nose.

Lawson quickly kissed it off her nose, then grinned. "I love you," he said abruptly.

"What did you say?"

He was surprised. He hadn't realized he'd spoken aloud, but her laughter had awoken something in him. He felt, for the first time, that they would make it after all. The year was almost over, and they were still aboveground, still safe. Edon would learn to forgive him, and Malcolm, who seemed weakened by his transformation, would grow stronger. The youngest boy's transition to life aboveground had not been an easy one, and Lawson worried that he had never fully crossed over, that when they'd made the break, Malcolm was too weak to undergo the change, and that part of his soul still remained back there. The youngest boy was always ill; his nose was always running; his back hurt; his eyes were dry.

Lawson had many worries: the biggest was the plight of the rest of the wolves in the underworld. Marrok would take care of them, he hoped. Since the five of them had returned to Hunting Valley, Lawson kept going back to check, visiting the place where they had landed when they first crossed from the underworld, but so far, no one had appeared in the glen. No other free wolves. Perhaps their plan had failed.

He didn't know if he loved Tala because of who she was or because she made him feel hopeful and made him forget. But he'd said it. *I love you.*

"Never mind." He shrugged.

She looked embarrassed for him.

But it was true. He loved her. He loved Tala and he wanted her to know it.

She said nothing more to him that day. She continued to eat the cream puff with a serious expression on her face, and then they went inside and she made them dinner, asking them gently to eat with the forks and knives as Arthur had taught them. The past year, Tala had been the linchpin of the family, holding them all together.

Maybe that was confusing him; maybe his feelings stemmed from her being crucial to their survival. In a way, he was glad she hadn't responded. Now he had some time to think about how he truly felt.

The pack settled into a routine. Lawson, Edon, and Rafe went to the big-box store early in the morning to pick up whatever odd jobs they could. Tala and Malcolm worked at home —Tala was in charge of housework and cooking, and Malcolm studied the books Arthur had given them to try to understand the extent and limitations of their power in this new world. Wolves were not immortal— they had not been bestowed with that gift—but they were long-lived and fast-healing and infinitely stronger than mortal men. They surprised construction crews with their ability to lift heavy objects; bags of cement that the men used to haul in wheelbarrows, Lawson, Edon, and Rafe tossed to each other like beanbags.

Every night Lawson would come home to find a mouthwatering concoction simmering on the stove while Malcolm talked excitedly about what he'd learned that day. The youngest spent most of his time working on a spell called the dogwood defense, one that he had read would protect the house from the hellhounds.

"We're hardly wizards," Edon would say, but then he'd

ruffle Malcolm's hair. He seemed to be less angry; sometimes he even spoke directly to Lawson, though never about anything significant. Most of the time it was to ask him to pass the salt at the dinner table. Lawson accepted that, hoped his brother would come around soon. He was tired of feeling guilty; besides, like he'd told Edon, he'd left the portal open for any others to cross over, and he meant to return if that didn't work, and when he did, he would bring all the wolves out of Hell with him.

Lawson wasn't sure if Tala was avoiding him, but they never seemed to be alone together. It was fine for now, because he had grown embarrassed about sharing his feelings for her. After all, if she felt the same way, wouldn't she say something? He tried to put her out of his mind, but every day there she was, with her shy smile, wearing her worn T-shirts that just skimmed her flat stomach, her faded jeans clinging to her slim figure, dark roots starting to show through her bright pink hair.

After a couple of weeks Malcolm decided he understood the spell well enough to attempt it. "I'm going to need everyone's help, though," he warned. He assigned everyone tasks: Edon was to carve the runes into the front door, Rafe was to gather the necessary herbs for the mixture, and Tala and Lawson would smear them around the house, making sure to leave no gaps.

Ringing the house with the herbal mixture Malcolm had created was painstaking work, much more so than Lawson had anticipated. They started on a night when he'd come home from work early. The sun was just starting to set, and the glowing pink matched Tala's hair. Lawson held an enormous vat of the foul-smelling, steaming stuff while Tala scooped it out and spread it on the ground. They worked in silence for what felt like hours before Tala announced that she needed a break.

"Sure," Lawson said. "Should we take a walk, stretch our legs a bit?"

"That sounds good. I could use a few minutes away from that smell."

They wandered away from the house, walking a few blocks in the twilight darkness without speaking. The air was cool, the sky clear. Lawson's hand brushed against hers a few times, but she didn't pull away. They hadn't been this close since the day she'd dyed her hair so long ago. There hadn't been a lot of opportunity to be alone on the run. Finally, he couldn't bear it, and he grabbed her hand and pulled her close to him. It was natural, instant; she fell into his arms and his lips were on hers. He barely had time to worry about whether she would respond before she started kissing him back. She tasted of bubble gum, sweet and soft.

She pulled away for a moment. She looked into his eyes in the darkness. "Do you remember what you said to me, a couple of weeks ago?"

"How could I possibly forget?"

"Did you mean it?"

Lawson stroked her cheek. "How could I not?"

"Well, I love you too," she whispered.

He grinned. "Of course you do." Feigning arrogance, but what he really felt was relief. And happiness.

Tala laughed. "Don't get cocky."

"Shut up and kiss me again," he said, running his hands under her jacket and layers of thin T-shirts, wanting to feel her skin on his, wanting to get even closer than they were.

She kissed him back for what seemed too short a time, then pulled away again. "Come on, we need to get back. We have to make sure the house is protected."

So they trudged back to the house and the dogwood spell. Lawson hoped Tala was paying close attention to the task at hand, because he couldn't concentrate on anything but this new feeling, this complete joy he'd never felt before. He hoped it never went away.

FOUR

One cold morning in December, Lawson woke to find the clock blinking 12:00 in faded red neon. He wandered out of his room to find Tala and his brothers sitting in the living room, staring at a dead television. "What happened?" he asked.

Edon shrugged. "Power's out. They must have figured out that no one really lives here. We should bail."

That was Edon's mantra, a never-ending drone: they needed to move on; if they stayed anywhere too long, the hounds would find them. But this time Lawson had resisted. The older boys had found real jobs at the town butcher shop; Mac was enrolled in a local public school. Best of all, he and Tala were often able to sneak away in the night and spend time together, even if they both knew it wasn't a good idea for things to go too far, for the boys to find out. Somehow, in the past month, he had ended up doing what he had sworn he would not. He was settling down; he was starting to feel comfortable. He had to admit—he was tired of running, tired of looking over his shoulder. Besides, there was still a chance—impossibly slim of course, but still there—that other wolves would somehow be able to escape through the portal he'd kept open, still a chance that Marrok would join them. He didn't want to leave just yet. Besides, with some work and ingenuity they'd made the abandoned house their own, with curtains and bookshelves and a kitchen that smelled like cinnamon and honey. Tomorrow they would run, always tomorrow.

"We're fine," Lawson said. "The dogwood spell will protect us."

"So you think. Do not forget that we are wolves, creatures bred for battle, not spells and potions," Edon argued.

"I think we should stay," Tala said, glancing meaningfully at Lawson.

"Me too," Rafe said. "I like it here."

"Well, if we're staying it would be nice to find some way to get the TV turned back on," Malcolm said.

"We'll check it out," Lawson said quickly, and motioned for Tala to follow him.

Once outside, they walked quickly out of the cul-de-sac toward a more populated area, where it soon became clear that the power was out in the whole town, not just in their house. Mystery solved, they had some time to be alone.

They found an empty bench and sat down. Lawson nuzzled Tala's neck. "Don't you think it's time to tell the boys about us?" he asked.

Tala shook her head. "I think we still need to wait. Rafe and Malcolm might not be ready, and Edon's still sad about Ahri."

It was true; the week before had been Ahramin's eighteenth moon day, and Edon had slipped into a funk that took days for him to shake out of. Lawson had been pretty depressed about it himself. They all knew what it meant. If Ahramin was still alive—and there was no guarantee the hounds had let her live after they escaped—she was surely a hound now, which meant they could never get her back. "I guess you're right," he said. "We'll just have to keep sneaking around."

"At least you saved Edon in time," Tala said. The oldest had made it to eighteen without being turned, and a wolf who managed to gain full form without being turned into a hellhound was said to be free forever. They were planning a surprise party for him that night, when he was no longer expecting it. Lawson had saved up some of his money to buy a small pig from the local butcher, and Rafe and Malcolm had set up a makeshift grill from a barrel and a window grate.

"We should get home and start dinner," Lawson said.

He spent the afternoon getting their food ready, thankful that the grill didn't require power. Edon seemed to appreciate the gesture and blew the candles of his homemade cake with a smile. After taking a bite of his slice, Malcolm suddenly announced that he had a stomach-ache. "You don't like the icing?" Tala joked.

Malcolm shook his head. He was thin and anemic-looking, his bony ribs poking through his thin T-shirt, and when he bent over, his shoulder blades protruded from his back like two small wings. Lawson had hoped that he'd start growing stronger, and had been slipping him extra food at meals, but nothing seemed to help.

"It must have been the pig—maybe I took it off the fire too early, it must have been too rare," Lawson said, blaming himself for Malcolm's stomach pains.

Tala helped Malcolm lie on the couch and placed a bowl under his head just as Malcolm vomited up his dinner. "We need a bucket! Now!" she yelled, and everyone scrambled to help.

Lawson was bringing a plastic bucket into the living room when he heard the knock at the door. Strange—no one had come to the house in the months they'd lived there.

Another knock. Sharper this time, more urgent.

"Who is it?" Edon asked, coming up beside him. He had a pinched, anxious look on his face, and Lawson knew it was because they didn't have any neighbors and no one knew they lived there. No one was supposed to know about this house. And now someone had come. But who?

He felt a growing trepidation in his chest, a tightening, a darkness. Lawson could feel the end coming, but he didn't want to acknowledge it yet, did not want to think about what it meant. It was nothing, just a stranger at the door, nobody, no one, it didn't mean anything, he told himself.

"Probably just the postman or something, I'll take care of it. Go see how Mac's doing," Lawson said. He'd taken on the role of alpha here, was used to giving orders, even to his older brother. Edon did as he was told.

Lawson's mind was racing in fear, but he was just nervous, he told himself. He pushed aside the metal shutter that covered the peephole window. It was dark, almost black, and he couldn't see anything. He wiped the glass with the edge of his shirt, and when he looked through again, he saw that the darkness had coalesced into a tall, thin form. A girl.

She stood in a seductive curve, her body sinuous and snakelike, her hand on her hip, jutted out like a fashion model. Her thick dark hair moved with a life of its own, swaying like satin ribbons around her face. Like Medusa, she had a cold and dangerous beauty, the beauty of a cobra or a lioness. She was dressed for battle, her black armor glinting in the twilight.

Lawson stood motionless at the door, unable to shake her gaze. His heart dropped into his stomach; he couldn't breathe.

No. No. Not now. No.

"Lawson!" Tala's voice snapped him out of his daze. "What's wrong? Who is it?"

When he didn't answer, she pushed him aside to look through the peephole. "Oh no," she whispered. "Lawson!" she cried. "DO SOMETHING!"

Her voice shook him into action. "THEY'RE HERE!" Lawson yelled. He could smell the hounds now. They'd be on them in an instant, coming from all directions, ducking through shadows and hiding in trees, making their way toward the house, bringing fire and ash.

"Make sure Edon doesn't see!" he said, grabbing

Tala's arm. Lawson began to barricade the door, tossing everything he could find against it—the chairs, the kitchen table. "Get everything we need! We're not coming back!"

Tala nodded and ran to secure the treasures of their pack.

"RAFE!" he cried. "Everyone to the middle, get ready to jump!"

"I've got it!" his brother yelled, hustling Malcolm toward the living room.

Hellhounds! Here!

Now!

He was so frightened he couldn't think, but he had to concentrate if he was going to get them all out of there, if they were going to survive this.

"It'll hold," Lawson said to Malcolm, who was shaking. "They can't get in the house."

Wordlessly, Tala pointed to the windows, her eyes wide with fright and despair.

He turned to see. Outside, flames ringed the perimeter. If the hounds couldn't enter the house, they would burn it to the ground.

FIVE

*T*he circle of flames was still far enough away that Lawson could see the snow-covered grass in between the fire and the house. But it wouldn't be long before the fire gained energy and started moving closer. All his planning, all his nights of worry wasted. The first home they'd ever had, about to be destroyed. His biggest fear was upon them, and he hated himself for thinking they'd been safe even for a moment. He slammed a fist hard against the wall.

Tala grabbed him by the shoulder. "Don't. We'll find another home. We built this one together, and we'll build another."

He swallowed hard, kissed her forehead brusquely. Thank god for Tala.

The scent of smoke made its way into the living room.

"Where's Edon?" Rafe asked.

Lawson knew where he was. He exchanged anguished looks with Tala. "I'll get him," she said.

"No—let me," Lawson said.

He ran to the kitchen.

Edon stood transfixed at the front door, peering out through the peephole. "You didn't tell me," he said without moving; he must have heard Lawson's footsteps behind him.

A low, throaty voice whispered from the doorway, *"Come to me, Edon . . . I've missed you so much."*

"It's not her," Lawson said. "Not really. Not anymore. You know that." He'd seen her eyes, seen how their blue had turned a deep reddish-black. "Ahri's one of them now." Ahramin had been turned. She was no longer a wolf; she walked upright; she carried a black sword; she was an extension of Romulus's will. A Hound of Hell.

"Edon, open the door so we can be together again . . . "

"I have to open it," Edon said.

"I can't let you do that." Lawson pushed Edon away from the door as Ahramin began pounding on it so hard that it made the walls shake and the light fixtures swing wildly. The pummeling was relentless, and it felt as if not

45

just the door but the whole house would collapse from the fury of her blows.

The girl's taunts turned to screams as the door held. "EDON!" she thundered as Lawson pulled his brother back into the living room. "EDON, IF YOU STILL LOVE ME, LET ME IN!"

Now that Edon was with them, the circle was complete. Edon sat dazed between Lawson and Rafe, who each held on to him in case he tried to make a run for the door.

"Can they follow us?" Malcolm asked, his eyes red and nose dripping.

"The hounds can't come through the portals," Lawson assured him. "At least the ones I make, I'm pretty sure." He didn't know how he knew; it was just instinct, but it felt right. "Close your eyes, and focus your hearts and minds."

Lawson waited until everyone had their eyes closed, and then began to open the portal with his mind. It would be a much more dangerous jump than their escape from the underworld; their souls would have to cross first and their bodies would follow, unlike in Hell, where their spirits and flesh were one. Around them, the windows cracked and glass shattered. Dust drifted down from the ceiling. The smell of smoke was overpowering. Outside the sky was an eerie charcoal, and smoke billowed around the house. He could see the first wisps of flame edging toward the window. And then it was upon them.

The room turned a dull orange as strips of flame shot across the old carpet. The heat was unbearable, but familiar: the black fire of Hell. The ceiling glistened and blistered.

Lawson felt the passage open, felt the universe expanding to create this space, a space for them to be safe. In his mind's eye, he watched as one by one the brothers crossed over, even as he kept his actual eyes open so he knew what was happening in the room.

Tala was waiting for him. *Go,* he urged her in his mind. *Go now.*

Only with you, she sent back. A charred beam fell from the ceiling and struck her. She fell backward, unconscious. Her mind lost its connection to his.

TALA! TALA, WAKE UP! WAKE UP! Lawson screamed as he stood at the border between the worlds. But there was no more time. Through the red-hot skeleton of the house, he could see dark figures gathered. Hellhounds, hunched in anticipation.

No. He couldn't lose her. He began to break the connection and the portal started to close. Their bodies were frozen in a circle, asleep and oblivious to the fire that raged around the room, as walls ripped open with flame.

His brothers began to yell. *LAWSON! HURRY!*

He reached out again for her mind, but he couldn't find her. For a few desperate seconds, there was nothing. Then, suddenly, the spark between them returned.

GO! Tala screamed. *GO! YOU DON'T HAVE TIME! LEAVE ME!*

I CAN'T, he screamed back. *I WON'T!*

The boys stood by the open passage, waiting while the room burned. Soon their bodies would be sacrificed to the flames and all would be lost. But still Lawson did not move. He was as paralyzed as Edon had been earlier at the door.

Tala, no ... I won't leave you the way Edon left Ahri. I can't let that happen. I won't.

Go ... Her voice was weaker now. But when she saw that he was hesitating, her voice recovered the ferocity he knew and loved so well. *Remember the pact! Go!*

Never!

But she pushed him away with her mind, and before he knew what was happening, he had joined his brothers on the other side. The portal continued to close and he heard her scream as a whip cracked in the flames.

TALA! Lawson's heart broke in anguish and fear. *TALA!*

In one instant the brothers were sitting in the burning living room; in the next, they had disappeared. The house shuddered, heaving its last gasp, and collapsed, the hounds storming the ashes of what they'd left behind. But Lawson and his pack were gone, save one.

SIX

*B*liss Llewellyn waited at the airport for Aunty Jane to pick her up from the bonding she'd just attended. Aunt Jane wasn't really her aunt; she was the latest incarnation of the *Pistis Sophia*, the Immortal Intelligence, what the Blue Bloods called the Watcher. She had been Lucifer's sister in an earlier cycle and since then had been destined to foresee the return of the Dark Prince from the underworld.

Bliss scanned the cars, looking for her aunt's Honda Civic. Sturdy and reliable, just like the form the Watcher had taken in this life, she thought. Jane Murray was a short, sensible-looking woman of late middle age who favored brightly colored wool cardigans, plaid skirts, and brown moccasins and was known to quote from Austen or Shakespeare when the mood struck.

She wondered why Jane's powers didn't extend to making them look more like relatives. Though the Watcher hadn't managed it the last time, either; when she'd taken the form of Bliss's sister Jordan, everyone always remarked they didn't look like sisters. Bliss herself was tall and rangy, with long, thick hair that fell in russet waves down her back. She'd even been a model once, back in New York, in another life. A life that had probably ended with the bonding she'd just left. When would she see her friends again? she lamented, thinking of Schuyler, Jack, and Oliver. She missed them so much already.

As Bliss wandered up and down the sidewalk outside the airport, her hand slipped under her shirt, and her fingers traced the long, ugly scar in the middle of her chest, a rumpled ridge of skin, bumpy and coarse. She tried not to pick at it, since it just made it worse when she did, but it was hard to stop.

The scar was a reminder of the girl she had been, dark history marked on her pale flesh. Lucifer's daughter. Devilspawn. Silver Blood: a corrupted vampire who fed on the souls of its own kind. A Dark Angel cursed to live the rest of her immortal life on earth, reincarnated through the cycles to perform her father's bidding. The Dark Prince had been using her as a way to seek revenge on his enemies, to wreak havoc and terror.

In the end she had managed to fight him and regain control of herself, her body, her memories. There was some cold comfort in knowing that it was all behind her, that there was nothing left of her father's malice except for a faded purple gash where she had plunged a knife into her own body rather than murder another innocent victim. Bliss had been ready to face death, ready to make the ultimate sacrifice. But she'd been blessed with another chance, a new life, a new way forward to redeem the past and forge a new identity.

But now that she was no longer Senator Llewellyn's eldest daughter, no longer a student at Duchesne, no longer a cheerleader from Texas, she didn't know who she was supposed to be. Was she still immortal? Her mother, Allegra Van Alen, had told her that she was human now, and that her true name was Lupus Theliel. Wolfsbane. But Allegra hadn't told her what it meant. She'd only told her to find the wolves. *They are demon fighters and we will need them in the final battle with the Silver Bloods,* she'd said. *Tame them. Bring them back to the fold.* She hadn't said anything else—not where to start, not where to go, nothing at all about how this task was to be accomplished. Bliss had managed to put it out of her mind so she could enjoy her friends' bonding, but now that she was home, she needed to get to work.

Finally, Aunt Jane pulled up to the curb. "Hop in," she said. "We've got a long drive ahead of us." Bliss thought about how much her friends would make fun of her if they could see her with this woman in this car.

"Where are we headed?" Bliss asked. Before she'd left for Italy, they had been investigating a case in Chicago, but Jane had told her to take a return flight directly to Ohio instead.

"Cleveland area."

"Hellhounds in Cleveland?" Bliss said, smirking a little.

"Maybe," Jane sighed. "Allegra must know something I do not if she thinks you can bring them back to our side. Hellhounds are uncontrollable, violent, and vicious, creatures of shadow. This is a dangerous proposition she has laid on your shoulders. We will have to exercise utmost care."

"But Allegra said they stood with the Blue Bloods once . . . that they've just been estranged," Bliss said.

Jane explained. "The hellhounds are Lucifer's Dogs. When the Dark Prince was known on earth as Emperor Caligula, they were his guards, the best soldiers in the vast Roman army. But the hounds turned tail, betraying their master to stand with the Blue Bloods during the Crisis in Rome, helping Michael to send the demon king back to the underworld. They disappeared soon after. Some say they were punished for their actions, and once again do Lucifer's bidding. The Repository isn't clear on this, though."

"Aunt Jane," Bliss said in a small voice. "If the hounds are with Lucifer, that means we'll have to go down to the underworld, doesn't it ... to find them? Down to the Ninth?" She shuddered at the thought of it. She had no desire to see her father again, much less to fight him for command of his dogs. Why had Allegra put this on her shoulders? More importantly, why had she accepted? She'd done it to repent for her actions, Bliss reminded herself, because whether she had been aware of it or not, she had been the vessel for her father's malevolent spirit in mid-world. She had accepted this task to clear her conscience, to do a bit of good in the face of impossible evil. She only hoped she was strong enough. She wasn't a vampire anymore—just a mortal girl now, with a middle-aged mortal to help her.

Her aunt's forehead crinkled. "I truly hope not. I hope that's not what Allegra had planned for us. Let's see what we can accomplish on this side of the fence for now."

Bliss exhaled.

"What's in Cleveland?" she asked.

"Not Cleveland exactly, but a place called Hunting Valley," Jane said. "There's a burnt house with a strange story. I think something happened there that might lead us to find what we seek."

SEVEN

"How was the bonding?" Jane asked as Bliss studied the papers on her lap and they drove deep into the night.

Bliss put down the newspaper clipping she was reading about the fire. She smiled a little, thinking of the happiness she had been part of so recently, which felt already as if it had happened many years before, as if the memory was already as worn as a sepia-tinged photograph. She thought of Schuyler's shining face and Jack's proud one. "It was wonderful," she said, blinking back tears, feeling a deep longing and an ache for something she knew she would never have. Love throughout eternity.

Jane reached over from the steering wheel and squeezed her arm in sympathy. "I know you're thinking about Dylan," she said. "But you were right to let him go."

Let him go ... an interesting choice of words. Bliss could never truly let Dylan Ward go. She thought of what he had done for her: kept her sane, given her the strength she needed to fight her father's spirit, to stand up to the Dark Prince. Her sacrifice had released her link to him— Dylan had moved on, gone to a better place—but she missed him with an ache that was a physical pain. She would never heal from it.

"One day, you will find a love as great as the one you two shared. You deserve happiness, my dear, and you will find it," said Jane.

Bliss sniffed, blinked back her tears. "I'm okay."

"I know you are." Jane smiled. "You are stronger than you know."

They drove the rest of the way in silence, and an hour later arrived at their destination. Jane pulled the rental car up to a police barricade around the remains of the burned-out house in the middle of the street. "I think this is it," Jane said. It was after midnight, and the streets were empty, the heavy cloak of darkness impenetrable. The only sound came from the crunching of their tires on the gravel. The night air was bracing cold.

They stepped out of the car. Bliss clicked on her flashlight and led the way. Once they'd reached what remained of the house, she swept the flashlight across what must have, at one time, been the living room. "What do you think?" she asked. True to the reports Jane had pulled up for her to read on the drive, only the front door was still standing. Otherwise, everything had burned to the ground, to ashes and dust, rubble and debris, covered by a light gray snow. "An accident? Arson? Or . . . ?"

"Not sure yet," Jane said. "Let's take a closer look around, see if we find anything odd."

Jane had printed a story about the burned house from a blog that documented supernatural phenomena. Those who'd witnessed it burning said they had heard terrible screaming, eerie roars, and manic howling from inside the house as the fire raged. But it was an abandoned home—no one was supposed to be living there—and after the fire had consumed everything, the police had found no human remains, no proof that anyone had even been in the house when it burned.

The fire had been written off as an accident—the electric company had forgotten to turn off the power and a utility cable had sparked during a blackout. That was all.

Maybe the police were right. Maybe nothing had

happened here. Maybe there was nothing to see, nothing here that would lead them to the hounds.

But Bliss kept staring at the door that was still standing, that hadn't burned. It was impossible that an entire house could burn down leaving just the one door. She could imagine it only if there had been some sort of spell, some kind of protection over the house that the fire had managed to extinguish, but only in part.

She shone her flashlight on the scarred face of the door, and up close she could see faint traces of writing on the burned wood. Runes of some kind, perhaps. Across the dark lot Jane sneezed from the dust. "Hamlet's ghost," she muttered, blowing her nose.

An accident, the official reports had concluded. Maybe the whole incident had been just a hoax. That was another possibility. There was no way to know for sure. No way to know, unless . . .

Bliss kept her light fixed on the door, slowly sweeping it down to the ground. She pushed some splintered wood off to the side with the edge of her sneaker.

There. She saw something.

She moved closer and shone her light directly on it, her heart beating in excitement at the heady rush of discovery.

"Aunt Jane!" she called. "Here!"

In the middle of the burned wood, half-buried in the ashes, was a black pebble that shone as bright as a glittering diamond. Bliss knew what it was immediately. The Heart of Stone—it was a remnant of the Black Fire of Hell.

Bliss clicked off her flashlight with some satisfaction. They were right. The hounds had been here.

EIGHT

*T*he former fire chief lived in a tidy house in a pleasant suburb, and as Bliss walked up the driveway she was struck by a feeling of homesickness so deep that she had to stop and catch her breath for a moment. The house was just an ordinary one-story home, a little cottage with pretty Christmas lights. She had grown up in a sprawling, elegant mansion in Houston and then a three-story penthouse in New York, but after traveling and then going on the road, she found something appealing about a home that was so orderly and neatly kept. *Home. Where is home now?* Bliss did not belong anywhere. She no longer had a home.

"It's all right," Jane said, squeezing her forearm. Her aunt always seemed to know what Bliss was thinking.

Bliss sighed as she rang the doorbell, steeling herself for what lay ahead. "He knows we're coming, right?" she asked.

"I spoke to him just this morning," Jane said. "He didn't seem to want to meet with us, but I can be very persuasive when I want to be."

Bliss smiled. She knew that without Jane she would have given up long before. As she rang the doorbell again, Bliss wondered what would happen if she did end up finding the hounds. Would they even give her a chance to speak? Would she have to strike a bargain of her own? Why had her mother sent her to them? And how would she ever get them to join their cause?

"Apathy is the glove in which evil slips its hand," Jane murmured.

Bliss frowned. "Shakespeare?"

"No, just something I read on the Internet the other day." Her aunt laughed. "A reminder to remain vigilant against our enemies."

Finally, a friendly older woman in a white apron opened the door. "So sorry—we were out back and didn't hear the bell. Come on in."

The former chief of the fire department had retired only a few weeks earlier. He was a tall, handsome older gentleman, deeply suntanned and courteous. His wife, the woman who'd let them inside, offered them cookies and tea, led them to a cozy room where they sat on flowered cushions. "So you guys are from New York, huh?" he asked, settling into his lounger. "Writers, they tell me." He sounded skeptical.

"Yes," Jane said brightly. "But don't worry; we don't work for the insurance company. We're writing a book about spontaneous combustion." It was the cover story they'd agreed on: they were researchers, writing a book about fire disasters. They hoped that knowing they were in the presence of academics, of writers, would put people at ease and would loosen their tongues. Everyone liked feeling important.

"We're here to ask about the fire out in Hunting Valley the other week," Bliss said.

He nodded. "Yep, that one. It was like nothing I'd ever seen. We couldn't put it out—not until every last bit of that place was burned to the ground, except the door, of course. When we got there, the walls were still standing but the door was locked from the inside, which happens, but when we hit it with the ram, it just wouldn't budge. The thing was wood, but it felt like steel. We couldn't break it. We couldn't get inside at all."

"Can you tell us again how the fire was started?"

"From the burn trailer it looked as if it had sprung around the house, all at once." He took a bite from a cookie and looked pensive. "Talk about spontaneous combustion. Water seemed to feed the flames instead of putting them out, and the smoke had a different odor. Weird."

"Like what?" Bliss asked.

"Pungent and strong, as if hell itself was burning." He frowned.

"There were eyewitness reports that they heard screaming . . . but you found no survivors?" Bliss asked.

He shook his head. "None."

"But the howling—" Bliss argued.

"Coyotes, most likely, there are some around the area," he said gruffly.

"Coyotes who walk upright? Right here it says someone saw great 'wolflike' silhouettes in the windows . . . " She held the printout in front of him but he dismissed it.

"People have vivid imaginations," he said, looking uncomfortable.

Bliss was disappointed; other than the Heart of Stone, she had been hoping to discover something more about the fire, something that could be a real clue to the hounds' whereabouts. She and Jane began to gather their things when the fire chief coughed and looked guiltily at them.

"Well, there was something," he said finally. He lit his pipe and the room filled with the sweet smell of tobacco.

Bliss and Jane exchanged looks, but neither of them said anything.

"We found something." He squirmed in his seat. "It's . . . difficult to talk about."

Bliss sat back down and leaned forward. "Tell us. You can tell us."

"Actually, not something . . . but someone. A girl." He closed his eyes, wincing at the memory. "The house burned right to the ground, piles of ashes everywhere—great mounds of it—you saw. It was a few days after the fire was out—me and my boys were doing cleanup when we saw her . . . a girl, buried under the ashes. Naked, covered in blood and dust. We thought she was dead."

"But she's not?" Bliss asked, hope thrumming in her chest. This was something—a beginning—a clue at last.

He shook his head. "Nope. She was breathing."

"Who was she?"

"Don't know. We had her checked out at the hospital . . . and it was the oddest thing . . . they said she was completely unharmed. No signs of physical injury, not one bruise, not one cut, not one burn. Just—covered in ashes. Ashes and blood." He took a puff from his pipe.

He hitched his pants, put down his pipe in the ashtray, stood, and left the room. When he came back after a few minutes, he was holding a notebook. It was covered in soot. "We also found this." He handed it to Bliss. "Will you take it? I don't like having it around." He seemed glad to be relieved of the burden.

"What happened to her? The girl you found?" *The girl covered in ashes and blood.*

"Mental hospital."

"Do you have the address?" asked Jane, ready with her pen.

He nodded. "I can get it."

This is it, Bliss thought, her excitement bubbling as she tucked the journal into her bag. Find the girl, Bliss knew, and she would find the hounds.

t. Bernadette's Psychiatric Clinic had taken great pains not to look like a mental asylum, to distance itself from the negative connotation of institutional sanatoriums: nightmarish loony bins where crazies were locked up and caged, left to sit in a mess of their own filth. It was a small four-story building located on a pretty hillside in a sleepy Cleveland suburb. There were no bars on the windows, there were no armed guards at the gates, and none of the nurses were named Ratched. The lobby was peaceful and cheerful, decorated in soothing pastel colors, and patients were allowed to wear their own clothes—none of that shuffling in hospital gowns and slippers.

The mental hospital looked innocuous enough, but

even so, when Bliss arrived in the afternoon, she could not help shuddering. In a past life, she had been sent to a place not unlike this one, and she could still remember the horror of that experience: the shackles and the tests, the buckets of cold water poured on her head during her ravings. The clinic was more like a college dormitory than a prison, but Bliss could bet that the windows at Case Western weren't built from two inches of shatterproof acrylic you couldn't break with a sledge-hammer.

She had left Jane back at their motel. For a moment she wondered whether she'd done the right thing; Jane had wanted to come, though she was too tired to protest when Bliss insisted she stay behind. But Bliss wanted to speak to the girl alone. It was her task, after all, her burden, to find the hounds.

"Sign here," the young guy at the desk said, pushing over a few papers.

Bliss scribbled on the page. "What's this?"

"Liability waiver. Means you can't sue the clinic if anything happens to you after seeing her. Or when you see her." He had a flat nasal accent, less midwestern than southern Appalachian, a real twang. Bliss had always thought of Ohio as the Midwest, like Kansas or Nebraska, but as they'd moved through the state, she'd discovered it was a real patchwork, a hodgepodge of big cities and dying steel towns, affluent suburbs that rivaled the toniest Westchester neighborhoods and a pretty rural countryside dotted with horse farms and lush green forests.

"I don't get it. What's going to happen?"

The orderly shrugged. "Not supposed to say, but see that lady sitting over there?"

Bliss nodded. There was a smiling middle-aged woman sitting by the window, talking softly to herself. Once in a while her whole face would twitch in a frightening spasm.

"Yeah, well, Thelma used to work here. Now she's a patient. She was your patient's nurse you know. Spent a week with her and went insane. And then there's the janitors . . . " He stopped without finishing the sentence. He only shook his head as he took the clipboard back and handed Bliss a visitor pass. "What do you want with her, anyway? You a reporter or something? Or family?"

Bliss shook her head. "Neither."

"Law enforcement?"

She shook her head again. The orderly finally stopped asking questions and they arrived at the girl's room. Bliss noticed immediately that there was something strange in the air. The feeling of death was all around, a grim darkness just behind the door. She did not feel frightened, only curious. She had lived with the spirit of Lucifer, so she knew what evil felt like. This was not the same. It was not the emerald-sharp feeling of hatred and spite; this was a feeling of dread and sloth, rot and ruin, misery and pain.

There was a small placard next to the door that read PATIENT: FIFTEEN.

"No name. *Nomen nescio*," the orderly said proudly, as if Bliss would question his knowledge of Latin. "The doctors thought they'd call her Nina but it didn't stick. She's not a Nina. So now we just call her by her room number. Fifteen."

Bliss peered through the peephole. Inside she saw a young girl perched at the edge of a long flat mattress. Her toes were curled around the bottom and dug into the foam. Her head hung down at an odd angle, swaying slightly as if broken. Her dark hair was shorn to the scalp, and Bliss felt a chill at seeing how skinny she was. Skeletal, with dark bruises on her arms.

The girl looked up straight at Bliss's eyes through the porthole and Bliss jumped back, startled by the girl's arresting stare. There was something wrong with the girl's eyes—Bliss was sure she saw a flash of crimson, but when she looked again, they were just a normal blue.

Just then the orderly unlocked the door. "She's all yours. Buzz when you're done."

"You're locking me in there . . . with her?"

"Rules. You signed the waiver."

Bliss kept her face impassive as the door locked noisily behind her. She leaned against the wall and crossed her arms. The girl never took her eyes off Bliss. "You're not scared of me," she whispered. Her voice was soft and weak.

"Should I be?" asked Bliss.

"They're all scared of me," she said softly, picking at the mattress. It was pocked with holes, Bliss saw, and lacked sheets, even a pillow.

"I heard." Bliss looked around the bare room. There was nothing in the space except for the mattress on the floor. No books, no pictures, not even a window. How long had the girl been living like this? "What's your name?"

"Fifteen." Her voice was quiet and subdued, defeated and sad.

"That's what they call you."

"That's right."

"What's your real name?"

"I don't know." She shook her head. "If I did I wouldn't be here."

"Why are you here?" Bliss checked the records. The fire had been only a month earlier, and the girl had been in the hospital since then, with little change or progress in her condition.

"There was a fire," the girl said. "It burned everything."

"You were in the house. What happened in that house? What happened to you?" Bliss asked.

The girl put clenched fists to her eyes. "I don't know. I don't remember."

"I want to help you," Bliss said. "Please."

"No one can help me. Not anymore."

"Look, I know what you're going through—I've been in a place like this. I was in a mental institution once. I know what it's like. You don't have to be here. You don't have to hide. Let me help you," Bliss said, fiddling with the charm around her neck that held the Heart of Stone. She had taken to wearing the dark talisman, wanting to keep it close, as if the glittering amulet could draw the hounds to her, help her on her journey. She moved closer to the girl. "I think I know what happened ... I know about the hounds. They're the ones that attacked you that night, isn't that right?"

At the mention of the hounds the girl scrambled to the far edge of the room, as far away from Bliss as possible. "I don't know what you're talking about. Leave me alone."

Bliss removed a dusty notebook from her bag and read from it. "'They will come for us, and when they do, we must be ready. We have protected the house, but will we be able to protect each other?'" She looked up at the girl. "This is your journal, isn't it? You wrote these words. What does it mean? The hounds were coming for you? But the house was protected somehow? Who are the others? Where are they?"

The girl shrugged.

"What did they want with you? Why did they come? How did you survive?"

"I don't know. I told you, I don't know what you're talking about," the girl said, growing more and more agitated.

"I was hoping you would help me . . . I am . . . looking for them. I need to reach the hounds," Bliss said, feeling as she uttered the words that it was a hopeless enterprise her mother had set her on.

The girl began to shake and rock back and forth, whimpering a little, like a wounded animal. "Get away from me . . . get away . . ."

"I'm sorry, I'm sorry . . . please believe me, I don't want to hurt you," Bliss said. "But I need to know about the hounds."

"The hounds!" the girl screamed suddenly, her eyes blazing, looking directly into Bliss's green ones. "Why do you seek the hounds? Beware! No one hunts the pack!"

They stared at each other in silence. Then the door opened. Time was up. Bliss left the room.

"So. What'd you think?" the orderly asked as they walked back to the lobby. "Hard nut to crack, right?"

Bliss did not answer, trying to convince herself that the girl in the room had no idea what she was talking about, that she just wanted to scare her. But Bliss had seen a lot in her lifetimes. She didn't scare that easily.

TEN

The girl's words had unnerved her, but Bliss managed to stay calm as she hurried across the hospital parking lot. She had faced monsters tougher than hounds. After all, they were merely her father's attack dogs and she wasn't going to be scared of a few mangy mutts no matter what that spooky-eyed girl said.

She dialed Jane's cell phone, needing to hear her aunt's friendly voice, and was disappointed when the call went to voice mail. Bliss left a message. "Hey, it's me. It's her all right, but she was uncooperative. Really uncooperative, if you know what I mean. I'll tell you more when I see you. I'm on my way back to the room. See you in a bit."

Traffic was slow and it was dark when Bliss rolled

into the crowded parking lot. The Bedside Inn was more apartment house than motel; too late they had discovered it served as a halfway station for people who couldn't make first and last months' rent or pass a credit check. When Bliss exited the elevator she found the doors to several rooms open on the floor, tenants chatting in bathrobes and wet hair, swapping stories and gossip. Kids ran from one room to the next as if the whole complex were their playground. She had experienced a moment of panic when she first saw the small, ugly room. There was graffiti on the pillows and the bedspread looked like it had last been cleaned in the Reagan era.

As Bliss made her way to her room, she nodded to her neighbors and leapt over their kneeling children, but the other tenants were cool to her; no one returned her nervous smile, and some looked outright hostile. It was with some relief that she finally reached her door. She knocked rather than using her key, just to let Jane know she was there. "Aunt Jane? It's me." She waited for her to open the door, but nothing happened. Could Jane still be sleeping?

She'd have to open the door herself. She slid the keycard into the reader and the light flashed green. She turned the lever and pushed the door open. The room was completely dark. She hated to wake up Aunt Jane, but she couldn't see a thing.

As soon as she turned on the light, she wished she hadn't. Furniture was tipped over, the room in disarray from a clear sign of a struggle, and the walls were raked by claw prints. There was no sign of Jane anywhere.

Bliss screamed.

No one hunts the pack, the broken girl at the asylum had warned.

A few hours later Bliss sat in her rental car in the motel parking lot, unable to move. None of the residents or staff at the motel had seen or heard anything. She had answered the questions posed by the police and the motel security and waited until they had cleared her alibi, thanks to the clinic's visitor log. Finally, the detectives dismissed her for the night. She meant to take a little break, maybe pick up something to eat, although she wasn't hungry. But she needed to get away from the chaos and fear for a bit, to be alone so she could think. She bit her fingernails one by one. The hounds knew she was looking for them. She was in danger unless she stopped, unless she gave up her pursuit.

They wanted her to give up, and they had taken Jane as a hostage. But why? Did they know Jane was the

Watcher? And what did the hounds know of Bliss's quest to find them?

Bliss knew she was on the right track; she was so close now. She had to keep going. She couldn't be scared, even if she had seen what they did. Her mother had given her a task; she had to see it through. She had known what she was getting into when she began. She had to keep searching for the hounds, and she couldn't leave Jane—her dearest friend in the world—in their hands, she could only hope she was still alive.

She looked out across the pale gray parking lot. The sun had vanished and its orange light was now replaced by a row of sodium lamps on tall posts. The lights cast a grainy yellow that made everything look as though it were one color: the trees, the distant traffic. A half mile away she could see a drugstore glowing brilliant white and a road trailing off to the west.

If she'd still had the vampire sight, she would have been able to see the curtains on the window of a house many miles away. But she was human now, with human limitations. She could no longer listen to a conversation conducted across the room; she could no longer lift objects five times her body weight. She could no longer do any of the things she had taken for granted when her blood was blue. Since the purging of her vampire self, she had not attempted to use any of her old powers. What was the use? She didn't want to look back and wish for something she could not have. But now she wondered if maybe some of her power had remained, if she could still enter the glom. *The hounds are creatures of shadow* ... Why hadn't she thought to find them that way before?

She closed her eyes and relaxed her muscles, letting her mind go blank, letting her consciousness expand beyond her and her physical limitations, allowing her to leave the tangible world. It felt as if she were slipping into a pool of warm water. When she opened her eyes, she was in the glom, in the world of twilight and specter, phantom and mirage.

Bliss moved cautiously through the empty landscape. The world of the glom had a slightly different tinge than she remembered. She did not know if it was because she was no longer a vampire, but for the first time, she felt alone and vulnerable.

Suddenly, a light in the glom, bright, like a spotlight, shone on her. She cowered from its brilliance, shielding her eyes. With a start, she saw there was a boy in front of her. He was dark-haired and handsome, with a high fore-head, a strong jaw, a fierce and noble visage—but his face was anguished. He stared at her—and she stared back.

Who are you?

Bliss wasn't sure who was speaking, him or her, but it was clear they both had the same question on their minds. She saw his gaze linger at the stone around her neck, his eyes growing hard, and she put up a hand to cover it, and before she knew what was happening—

She was thrown backward and when she recovered she saw she was somewhere else. A butcher shop. She saw the meat hanging on hooks, the white paper, the bloody shanks. Then a wolf stalked out of the darkness. A silver wolf with flat yellow eyes.

It was a hellhound; she was sure of it.

It leapt at her and Bliss felt herself pushed out of the glom and back into the real world, shaking and struggling to breathe.

She was still in the motel parking lot; next to her a family was unloading their luggage from a minivan.

Who was that boy? What was that light? No time to think about that now. The glom had given her the answer she needed. It had shown her a Hound of Hell. She had spied the address of the butcher shop on a paper bag. She would go there immediately to find the hound. She would follow wherever it led. And if she discovered Hell, well, she had already been there once.

PART TWO

To murder my love is a crime
But will you still love
A man out of time

Elvis Costello, "Man Out Of Time"

The Trials

It was the dawn before the trials. He crept back into the room through the hole he'd made in the wall. The masters didn't know he could do that. Escape. Push things around with his mind. Create a space where there wasn't any. They didn't know that he could travel outside the dens, that once he had even gotten all the way out to the first circle, as far as the borderlands, before turning back. The masters locked them in at night, steel meeting steel with a heavy clang. It didn't matter. He could go anywhere he wanted. But there were the others to think about, and he couldn't leave them behind.

The next day would mark him as the finest warrior of the pack. If he succeeded in besting his opponent, he would call the pack his own. He would be alpha. He had prepared for this all his short life.

All around, he could hear the sounds of his brothers sleeping next to him: their steady breathing, Rafe's gentle snore, Edon's nose *whistle, Mac's quiet whimpers.* He looked up at the ceiling, feeling ill. *It was hot in the room.* He couldn't sleep, thinking about the next day and what it would bring.

The next day began the same as any other, with rations at the commons, a plain, thick gruel that tasted and felt like lead. Fuel. He barely touched his plate; he saw his youngest brother eyeing it and pushed it toward him. *There was never enough; the masters kept them fed but not satiated—they liked them lean, hungry, all the better for fighting.* He watched Mac finish the rest.

Nerves? *Edon asked.*

He shrugged. Maybe.

You'll be good. *Mac reassured him.* They don't have anyone who can fight you. *The youngest wolf had taken it upon himself to be his trainer, his coach. All the days leading up to this one, Mac had been on the sidelines, yelping, cheering him on, helping devise strategy, teaching him how to breathe when he had blood in his mouth, when all the muscles in his body were screaming for release, advising him how to push through the pain to victory.*

They ate in silence and he watched.

Luck. *Edon nosed him.*

Ditto, *Rafe added, doing the same.*

He growled his thanks. This was it. This was what he had been waiting for. This was what he'd planned, what he'd trained to do. He would win and he would lead, or he would die.

*

The fight was short and brutal.

Over almost before it began.

He lay facedown in the arena, blood dripping into his eyes, blood pouring out of his wounds, blood everywhere on the sandy floor of the pit.

The blood was thick and he couldn't see. Why was he still alive? He should be dead. He had lost. He was beaten. He was no alpha.

This wasn't the way it was supposed to happen.

It was quiet in the arena. He was alone, he was sure. He was afraid to move. What if they thought he was dead? What if someone speared him with a lance if he turned over? He lay still, tasting his blood, metal and salt on his tongue. His body would heal, but for now he was in shock.

During the battle he had heard the jeers of the crowd, felt the disappointment of his den-mates, seen the fear in his brothers' eyes. They couldn't bear to watch. His talent had forsaken him. He couldn't use it. He floundered from the beginning and he knew it was the end. His end.

Why was he still alive?

Romulus raised his thumb, *someone answered. He hadn't realized anyone could hear him.*

It was tradition to wait at the end of a battle for the general's approval before the winner unleashed the death blow. In all the years, in all the centuries of the pit, no one had ever been spared. Not one.

The crowd lusted for death, and death was given to them. He thought death would be sweet compared with what he was feeling now.

But Romulus had raised his thumb. He had let him live.

Don't try to move. You'll only feel worse.

He felt a soft tongue on his brow, mopping up the blood, wiping off the salt and the crust and the grit and the sand that had embedded in *his skin.*

He turned over and finally he was able to open his eyes. There was a wolf kneeling in front of him, cleaning his wounds. He recognized her. She was from his den. A plain brown wolf with kind blue eyes.

Tala.

Yes.

Tala. She was just one more cub in the litter. He did not remember seeing her at the usual watering holes where they gathered. What passed for courtship among their kind was spontaneous, physical, instant. Wolves were able to breed until they were turned, but their offspring was not theirs to raise; cubs were turned over to the masters and assigned to a den. Once they were hounds, they were infertile, soulless killing machines. When it was clear that he would be the one most likely to lead the pack, there had been many who'd wanted to share his bed, but he had resisted. He would breed no cubs for the masters' kennels. He would not give them more wolves to turn. He had succumbed to temptation only once and had vowed never to do so again.

Tala continued to clean his wounds and she pushed him to his feet. She was surprisingly strong for how small she was.

Thank you.

She nodded.

He was shaking from fear, he realized; he was still so afraid. What if the masters returned? What if they took him away? He thought of everything he and Marrok had planned—if he was killed, it would all be for nothing.

He cringed at the sound of footsteps, but Tala shook her head.

They're not coming back. Not yet.

What's going to happen to me?

Nothing. Do not worry. I won't let anything happen to you, I am here.

He wanted to believe her. He knew she was lying to make him feel better. He would be killed, tossed into the Black Fire, left to burn.

But what if he was allowed to live? What then? How could he face his den? His brothers? After this colossal failure? Where would he rank in the pack now?

The taste of defeat was new, unexpected, raw.

How could this happen? *He anguished.*

You let her win.

She knew.

He did not argue.

The masters did not come that day; he was not speared and

thrown into the fire. Tala helped him back to their den. Life went on as usual, until their escape.

He wouldn't fall in love with Tala until they were on the other side, until they were free. But later he thought that maybe he had loved her even before. That day in the arena, when he had been defeated for the first time, when he was near death, when she had brought him back to life.

ELEVEN

Malcolm was sick and Lawson was glad. It meant that they were on the right track, that the hounds were nearby, and that meant they were close to finding the oculus. They were back in Hunting Valley, after having been gone for almost a month following the attack. When they crossed the portal, they had emerged somewhere near the coast, in a small town in Maine. They had learned their lesson by staying in Hunting Valley too long. They'd returned to Ohio the night before to find that even Arthur had changed domicile; the attack had unnerved him and he was living in a cave, of all things. Lawson thought it was a good idea. Stone was fireproof at least. They'd bunked there for the day, and upon moonrise had taken off for their destination, Malcolm's stomach acting as a guide.

"You all right?" Lawson asked from the driver's seat.

"No. Pull over," Malcolm said urgently. The minute Lawson stopped the car, Malcolm yanked open the door, making horrible regurgitating noises.

"Try not to hurl all over the car, all right? Took a lot of work getting this for nothing," Lawson said, keeping his voice light. He'd stolen the car, of course; they could never have afforded it otherwise. They'd have to lose it in a week or two, or once someone got suspicious about that old license plate he'd bolted on it.

Malcolm gave a hollow laugh, leaned over, and threw up his dinner all over the gravel, trying not to get any vomit in their new car.

Rafe gave his brother a sympathetic pat on the back. "Let it out, let it out."

"You're killing him, you know," said Edon from the passenger seat.

"Mac?" Lawson asked. "You sure you can do this? We don't have to," he said, although he knew it was a lie.

Malcolm knew it too. "I'm okay," he said, wiping his mouth with his sleeve. He sat up straighter, regained his spirit. "Keep your eyes on the road, hotshot. Don't worry about me."

"Maybe put your seat belt on too while you're at it," Edon said. It was pitch black outside and Lawson was cruising at just over ninety, headlights off. "No one minds if you hurt yourself, but you might plow into one of us on your way out the windshield. We'd rather not pick glass out of our hair."

Lawson grunted. He gazed at the endless black pavement, no streetlights, just the dark of the sky and the endless road. He drove fast because it was fun and he could always talk his way out of a ticket, and he drove without headlights because it was easier to see hellhounds in the dark.

The oculus couldn't be too far now if Malcolm was so ill. The youngest could sense the hounds' presence, they'd learned; his stomach acted as an alarm that the hounds were near. It had kept them one step ahead of their pursuers.

When they lost Tala, for a while it had seemed they had lost Lawson too. His brothers knew the reason—he and Tala hadn't fooled anybody with their sneaking around. He had shut down, just like Edon had after their escape, if not worse. He did not speak, did not eat; he was barely functioning. His heart was shattered. It was torture not knowing what had befallen Tala, whether she had been killed immediately upon capture, or whether the hounds had let her live. Even if they had kept her alive, it was only a few weeks now to her eighteenth moon day, and he had seen what had happened to Ahramin.

There was little hope of executing a rescue operation. Hell was vast and infinite; Tala could be anywhere. He could spend the rest of his life looking and he would never find her. As the days went by, there was even less chance of finding her alive and unchanged.

She was gone, and that was it.

Until . . .

A few days earlier Malcolm had woken screaming from his sleep, sweat running down his face. "It's *him*, I can see him!" The "him" was Romulus, of course. The Great Beast of Hell was ever in their minds.

"You saw Romulus? Where?" Edon demanded, his voice rising in panic.

"It looked like he was in the moon," Malcolm said. "He was speaking to someone."

"An oculus," Edon said, wary. He explained that the *obscura luminis* were beacons that shone in the glom, *the dark lights*, which the wolves had used thousands of years earlier, during the days of the old empire, to communicate over vast distances. They were scattered all over the globe and the underworld, had been used by the Praetorian Guard to keep track of the packs as they roamed across the universe, but the oculi had been dark for centuries. Now one was lit, and possibly working.

"Where?" Lawson asked.

Malcolm shut his eyes, concentrating. "It looked like it was in that place we first appeared, when we arrived here. That open meadow, surrounded by hills in the valley."

An oculus. Lawson felt the first flash of hope rise in his chest. "I can use it, I can use the oculus to find Tala. It can show me where she is, where they're holding her."

"No!"

Lawson looked at Edon as if he were a stranger. "No?"

Edon glared at him. "If you use the oculus, you could risk revealing our location to Romulus! Don't you see that? You would put us all in danger."

"I won't—I can do it—I know I can. I'll be quick, I promise. Nothing will happen." He couldn't give up on Tala, not yet. She might still be alive, and if she was, he couldn't leave her to that dark fate; he owed her that much. He thought of his love, the girl with the bright pink hair and the shy smile who sang softly to herself while she went about her chores. He could still see her, lying next to him in bed, could still feel her sweet breath on his cheek.

"Edon—please. Let me do this thing," he'd begged. He knew Malcolm and Rafe would follow, and it was Edon he had to convince.

"No, Lawson. You are a fool if you think you can get her back. It's over. She's gone. You must accept your loss as I have," he said.

"No." He felt a coldness inside him as he looked at his brother. Lawson had not wanted to admit it before, but in his heart, he judged Edon as weak for not having returned to Hell to rescue Ahramin. Weak for letting her sacrifice herself while he ran to freedom. He'd pitied Edon then, and he hated him for it now. That Edon no longer had any hope did not mean it was the same for him.

Tala might still be alive. Alive and unturned. Still the wolf he loved. There was hope. There was an oculus. It would show him where she was and he would get her back. Or he would die trying. Since he'd lost her, Lawson had all but forgotten about Marrok, and the rest of his brothers and sisters in the underworld; only Tala mattered for now.

In the end, Edon had crumbled, as Lawson had known he would. But as they drove toward the oculus, Lawson felt a stab of guilt. He was running in the dark—literally and figuratively. He had sworn to protect the pack and yet here he was, leading them straight to danger. Edon said the oculus was sure to be guarded by hounds, and Malcolm's queasy stomach confirmed this. Even Arthur had not approved of the idea.

"Look, I didn't ask for you guys to come with me," Lawson grumbled now. "I told you I could handle it myself."

"Sure you can, man," Rafe said from the back. "But why should we let you have all the fun?"

"We're only here because of you. Remember that," Edon said. *Remember that you are risking our freedom for your happiness.*

What if Edon was right? What if Tala was already dead? What if Romulus found them through the oculus? What then? If he failed to use the oculus without being seen, the hounds would be upon them and they would all be dragged back down to Hell, and all would be for naught.

"Fine," he said. "Fine. You win." He began to turn the wheel around. He was asking too much. He would not be able to bear it if one of his brothers lost his life in an effort to save Tala's. Edon was right—this was likely to put them all back in chains.

"No," Malcolm said from the backseat, his voice hoarse. "We need to go on. We already took a vote. We're going to the oculus. We told Lawson we'd help him and we will."

Lawson raised his eyebrow at his older brother, and for a moment, the tension in the car was strung as tightly as a kite string.

Finally, Edon threw up his hands. "Just make it quick, all right?"

"No one's faster than me." Lawson grinned as the car shot forward in the night.

TWELVE

"Oh god," Malcolm gurgled, clutching his middle.

Lawson let off the gas. "How far?"

The deathly ill look on the younger boy's face told him all he needed to know. He put the car in neutral and let it roll. With the lights off and the engine out of gear, the car whistled quietly down the steep incline like a sailboat cruising on smooth black water. Lawson watched and listened as they drifted down the slope, studying the trees and tall grasses for any sign of movement. Crickets chirped and fireflies flickered in the distance.

The car slowed until it stopped, and Lawson turned off the engine.

"Where's the guard? Do you see them?" he asked.

Rafe swept the landscape with a pair of binoculars. "They're on patrol, on the other side of the ridge."

"There," Edon said quietly, pointing to a blinking light through the trees.

"I see it." Lawson nodded. "Stay in the car," he told Malcolm. "The rest of you, come with me—you wanted to help, so you know the drill. If you get into trouble, let me deal with them. Don't be a hero. Leave them to me."

"Sure thing." Rafe smiled, his sleepy eyes lighting up. "You get your ass kicked, we'll stay out of it. Let them slap you around a little."

Lawson stretched his neck and cracked his back, flexing his arm muscles, preparing himself for what lay ahead. "I just want to have a little chat. It'll be a cakewalk, I promise." He slammed the door and led the rest of the team closer to the light. No time to think of whether this was the right thing to do now. He just had to make it through the next few minutes. He had to concentrate. Get in and out before those hounds nearby caught their scent. "Ready?" he asked, preparing the boys for the ritual.

One by one the brothers whispered the words that bound them, the pact they had sworn to each other. As they recited their words, a small blue crescent appeared on each of their faces. The sigil of their pack, the pulsing sickle throbbed in time with the beating of their hearts, giving testament to the bond they shared. When the testimony was over, the blue marks faded from their cheeks.

"All right, then," Lawson said, preparing himself for battle.

Next to him, his brothers were doing the same, their shoulders squared, blood pumping, eyes narrowed to squints, ready to attack if hounds appeared. Ready to fight. Edon balled his fists while Rafe cracked his knuckles. They were trained warriors, lean and ready.

The light blinked on and off through the dense forest of trees. Lawson struck out ahead, Edon next, and Rafe pulling up the rear. They fanned out in a triangular formation, keeping just enough distance from each other that they could easily come to each other's defense while having space to get away so that not all of them would be captured if it came down to that.

Lawson left his brothers at the base of the hill and followed a trail to the top until he was standing just outside a dim pool of light centered in a clearing of the trees. Tall shadows radiated in all directions from the circle. The ground was newly cleared, covered with a fresh bed of leaves and ringed with tree stumps.

"I'm going in," he called.

"Go on, then," Edon said.

"Get it over with," added Rafe.

"Relax," Lawson chided. The hounds were far enough away. In the silence he could hear only the rustling of the leaves and the soft quiet slithering of snakes in the moss, the sniffing and scratching of woodland animals.

He stepped into the light of the oculus. Edon had briefed him on how to use it, and it sounded simple enough. Let the light shine on him, and then command it to show him what he wanted to see.

When he entered, the forest and hill and trees disappeared, and his vision filled with a blazing light, white-hot like the center of a star. Lawson shielded his eyes and blinked. At first he was dazzled by the light, surrounded and engulfed by the white glow, but then he felt a familiar sensation and he realized that it was not light he was seeing at all, but its polar opposite. The beacon was made from a darkness that was complete, the darkness of the abyss, his former home. He had grown unused to it since their escape.

Inside the oculus he was overwhelmed by images from every place and time; he could see into the past and the present, into all corners of the universe. He had to make it stop, make it show him what he wanted to see, what he needed to see.

"Show me my mate," he ordered. "Tala of the Wolves, Born of the Underworld, Slave to None."

The whirring images stopped and a vision of a girl appeared.

Was it Tala? Lawson couldn't tell. He squinted into the light. If only the oculus would show him more—but the image remained vague and fuzzy. He was beginning to feel frustrated when it suddenly snapped into focus. He took a sharp breath. There was a girl in front of him. But she was definitely not Tala.

She was beautiful, though, with curly red hair and green eyes. She had a forthright, arresting grace about her, but her eyes looked a bit sad, as if she had been through some hardship.

She stared at him.

"Who are you?" he whispered. Then he noticed the amulet around her neck. The Heart of Stone. She carried the Black Fire of Hell. He jerked away from her, his mind racing. She was not a hound, he knew that much— her eyes were green, not crimson—but the charm she wore marked her as one of the underworld. A spy! Romulus's spy! She had to be a human tracker—he'd heard the masters sometimes used Red Bloods as eyes and ears aboveground.

Lawson cursed under his breath. She had seen him—

looked directly at him. He couldn't panic. He had to do something—what? If she was a spy, then let her come to them—*Let her find us,* he thought. She was close by—he could sense her presence—perhaps only a few miles away.

He sent her a vision of the butcher shop, let her see him as a wolf. He felt her satisfaction. He was right, then. She was looking for them. That much was clear. She answered to Romulus. He released her from his vision.

The darkness returned and the oculus went black. Why had it shown her to him? To warn him? It had to be. But where was Tala? The oculus hadn't given him the answer he sought.

Lawson didn't know what to do. He was wasting time; the longer he stayed in the light of the oculus, the greater the risk that Romulus would see him there. He hesitated, and while he was vacillating, the oculus came back to life and a low, powerful voice rumbled from hidden depths.

"Speak your name, hound." It was a command. Romulus.

Lawson backed away from the light, trying not to panic. The voice filled him with fear and loathing, and it took all his strength not to run. So far, it seemed that Romulus had not recognized him. But he had to get out of there.

"Speak your name."

Think ... He had to say something ... or it would become suspicious ... he could not stall for longer ... he had to do something ... say something ... he waited too long ...

The oculus went dark and as the earth opened up beneath him, he was thrown into the void.

THIRTEEN

*L*awson was falling, tumbling through a dark cavern filled with sharp rock, and when he landed, he crashed hard on the stone ground.

"Ugh," he groaned. He heard the shuffling of feet and looked up to see his brothers standing at the edge of the pit, looking down at him.

"Oh great, just great," Edon said when he saw Lawson lying there. "Did you have to get caught? Did you do this on purpose?"

"Not funny," Lawson said, trying to stand up. Thank goodness his body healed quickly.

"Ah, you'll survive," Rafe said.

"I don't think I've survived this yet, genius," Lawson snapped. "Come on, guys, a hand?" He knew his brothers were enjoying this a little too much. At least he was upright. Now he just needed to get out of this hole. "Where's Mac?"

"You dead yet?" Malcolm asked, peering over the edge.

"I keep trying, but the universe won't seem to oblige. Any ideas on how I can get out of this one?"

Malcolm was quiet for a moment. He disappeared from the edge of the pit only to return a moment later with a broken branch. "Rafe, can you take this? I'm not sure I can support his weight."

Rafe took the branch and held it over the side. "Lawson, can you climb up some of those rocks and then grab hold of this?"

Lawson flexed his arms and legs. Nothing seemed broken, and his bruises would fade quickly. He scaled the walls of the cavern and then grabbed the branch, letting Rafe pull him to freedom.

"We have to get out of here," he said. "Mac, how you feeling?"

"Bad," Malcolm said, and Lawson could see his face was pale, greenish. "They're heading back to the oculus now. A small unit, two or three." Malcolm shook his head and clutched his stomach. "I think I need to puke."

Edon hustled them to the car. "No time. Let's go, let's go. I'm driving."

Lawson didn't argue and took the backseat next to Malcolm. Edon drove the car quietly and carefully back down the dirt road, then gunned the engine once they were out on the highway.

"So what did you see in there?" Malcolm asked when they had put some miles between them and the oculus. The youngest boy had color back in his cheeks, a good sign.

"I heard Romulus," he finally admitted.

"Are you sure?" Malcolm asked, paling at the name of their fearsome general.

Edon whipped around. He slammed his hand on the steering wheel. "Did he see you? Did he know you were in the oculus?"

"I don't think so. He kept asking my name. I don't think he recognized me," Lawson said. He hung his head. "You were right, it was a mistake to come."

"Whether or not he knew who you were, we've got to move." Edon glowered.

"Not yet," Lawson said. "There's something else." He told them about the girl he'd seen, the one with the brilliant red hair and sad green eyes, the tracker, Romulus's spy. "I sent her an image of the butcher shop. She's going there now. Take me there."

"You want her to find us?" Malcolm gaped.

"I want her to find me," Lawson said smoothly.

"Why?"

"Isn't it obvious?" Rafe asked, looking solemn.

"Leave her to me," Lawson said, his jaw set, his heart burning with hatred. "I'll take care of her."

"What about Tala?" Malcolm wanted to know.

"I don't know. The oculus didn't show me Tala." He gazed out the window, his heartbeat finally slowing to a regular rhythm although his back still ached. He had wanted to see her so badly, but the oculus had shown him someone else. The red-haired spy. He clenched and unclenched his fist. He had lured the spy to the butcher shop, where she would meet her death.

FOURTEEN

*T*he shadows made everything look larger and smell worse. Styrofoam platters and massive rolls of wax paper were stacked on the counters. Hooks from empty meat racks hung from the ceiling, their crooked silhouettes looking even more ominous in the moonlight. Tacked on the brick walls were charts mapping animal bodies, depicting the various primal cuts. Shoulder. Chuck. Loin. Near the entrance were two large glass counters full of steaks and chops wrapped in cellophane.

Bliss took a deep breath and held it for as long as she could, willing her tense muscles calm. She had found the right butcher shop, had driven right up to it, and had seen from the corner of her eye the silver wolf in the shadows, had watched its arched, furry body slink through the back door, and had followed it inside.

She crept as quietly as she could across the wet stone floor. It was lurking somewhere within the darkness, waiting. Her eyes caught a flicker of light in the distance. In the back she noticed the door to the meat locker was open, revealing a carcass swaying like an inverted pendulum. So that was why the room smelled of blood.

She closed her eyes so she could hear. Concentrate. She pinched her nose. The smell was distracting. When Lucifer had taken over her body and had been her only contact to the outside, she'd found she could listen better if she closed her eyes and withdrew from her other senses. So even if she was only human, she was used to the dark. Lucifer had taught her that. She heard a clock tick, the sound of a hook grinding against a chain, the soft click of claws against the concrete—the beast, stirring ... and then there, barely perceptible, was the sound of someone else breathing. There was someone else in the room. Someone other than the creature. But where? And who?

The horrible clicking grew louder, and Bliss heard a snarl, deep and primeval and vicious, and then the sound of breathing became louder, more desperate—then, suddenly, a scream from beyond the doorway. Bliss leapt from her hiding place and ran toward it.

Clang!

A knife made a loud noise as it hit the concrete to her right. She swiveled in its direction, then stopped. The knife was a ruse, a distraction. The hound was behind her now; it was trying to steer her away from the door. She could see it watching her from the shadows, its yellow eyes burning. Did it think she was that stupid? She might not have her vampire abilities anymore—but it didn't mean she was completely useless. She was still fast. She was still coordinated. She still had the speed and skill of a trained killer.

The beast snorted and raked its claws across the concrete. It was angry and getting ready to jump. Bliss figured it was now or never. She pushed her way toward the open door, clambering onto a table and spraying a dozen knives across the room. The wolf leapt but she was faster, and when she reached the oversized steel door, she grabbed the handle and, using its weight as a pivot, swung around so that she pulled it closed behind her. The freezer slammed shut with a thick, wet sucking sound that made her wonder if this was a good idea. How much air was in here? No time to worry about that now. She picked up a couple of knives that had fallen to the floor, and jammed one into the lock to keep it closed while slipping the other into her back pocket.

She could hear the creature throwing its weight against the bolted door, making the archway shake. It was larger and more dangerous than she had thought. Tame the hounds? She would be lucky if she got out of there alive.

She looked around. There were a dozen or so carcasses hanging from the ceiling. The air was rancid, metallic. She pushed her way through the animal corpses to the back of the room, toward the sound of ragged breathing.

On the floor of the meat locker lay a boy, no older than she was, chained to the back wall of the freezer. Next to him were a cutting board and a band saw. A meat hook, crusted with blood and rust, swung above his head. The tiled walls were splattered a deep shade of scarlet. The boy's skin was blue, his hair caked with filth . . . there were ugly red marks around his wrists and neck, where he was bound with heavy iron shackles. Dear god, what was going on here? Bliss wondered, her stomach churning . . . If this was what they did to their victims . . . she didn't want to think about what Jane was going through and hoped that Jane was still alive . . .

Bliss shivered, goose bumps appearing on her skin. Now that she wasn't a vampire, her body did not control its temperature as well as it used to. But was it the fright or the cold that had caused the rows of tiny bumps?

She bent down to touch the boy's face. It was still warm, at least. She placed a tender hand on his bony shoulder. "You're going to be okay," she told him, and wondered if she was also telling herself the same thing.

"Yes, but you're not." His eyes came alive then, and before Bliss could blink, the boy had wrapped his fist around her neck and pinned her to the floor, his knees locking against her waist and keeping her arms away from her body. His shackles, Bliss could see now, had not been locked.

"Who are you?" she asked, spitting out the words with difficulty, recoiling from the boy's viselike grip. Bliss turned to her assailant, surprised to find she had seen his face before. He was the boy she'd seen in the glom. The boy with the same flat yellow eyes as those of the hound she had been tracking.

"I think the correct question is, who are you?" His voice was low and tinged with malice. "You are from the underworld, do not deny it, why else would you carry this?" he said, tugging the thin leather rope that held the Heart of Stone. "You are one of Romulus's spies!"

"I have no idea what you're talking about, but if you think I'm going down like Jane, you're wrong," she said, stretching her arm and reaching into her back pocket for her hidden blade. Her fingers shaking as she struggled to get a handle on it, she wriggled it out without him seeing, her heart beating too fast.

Quick as a flash, she stabbed him in the thigh with the knife.

He yelled in pain and she was able to push him off her and scramble away, but her freedom was short-lived, as she felt his hand wrap around her ankle and pull her back to him.

She screamed and kicked, thrashing wildly to get away, but he was too strong. Before she knew what was happening, he had his hands wrapped around her throat again.

He began to squeeze the breath out of her and she panicked, struggling and fighting to breathe; it was use-less—he was so much stronger—but as she looked into the boy's curiously yellow eyes, an image flashed in her mind.

She saw Lucifer—her father—standing inside an elaborate palace, surrounded by magnificent columns of gold. A cast of thousands was gathered, and Lucifer stood at the top of a marble staircase, looking down at a creature of exquisite beauty. It was a man, but it was taller than a human male, with a certain otherworldly magnificence, wild-eyed and ferocious, with the same dazzling golden eyes.

The image did not come from her memory but from Lucifer's. When she had been captive to his spirit, when he had taken over her soul, fragments of his memories had drifted into her consciousness. Triggered by random events, memories she'd never had would suddenly pop into her mind. She closed her eyes to recall the scene once more. She could hear Lucifer speak. The language was unfamiliar, its words harsh and convoluted, but she knew she could speak them as if they were her own.

"Release me!" she cried in that strange and foreign tongue. The room froze as the boy stared at her in surprise. He eased his grip and fell away, gaping at her in amazement and confusion, as if he could not quite understand why he had let her go.

But it was too late—she'd lost too much oxygen; everything went black—and Bliss felt the life seep out of her.

awson steered the car away from the butcher shop, through the busy streets of town and out to the old gravel roads. The rumble of the tires against the rock was a comforting noise, like the soft roar of ocean waves, and if he wasn't careful, it would lull him to sleep. The girl was still passed out on the backseat. Malcolm said she was fine, he'd felt her pulse, and she would wake soon enough. The youngest was sitting next to her, monitoring her progress. He'd learned her name from her identification card in her purse.

The trap had worked. Malcolm had shifted, the markings of his wolf form the closest to Lawson's, and led her inside the shop, where Lawson lay in wait. He'd sent Edon and Rafe ahead to protect Arthur, in case she came with a pack of hounds. But now Lawson hoped he hadn't done much damage. He'd meant to kill her, but when she spoke to him in the ancient language of the wolves, the words that had been lost to them since Lucifer's curse, he knew she was not an enemy. Speaking *Hroll* was punishable by death. So it meant that maybe, just maybe, Bliss Llewellyn was even a friend.

His mind raced. If she was not one of Romulus's trackers, what did she want? Why was she looking for them? Why had the oculus shown him her image? It slowly dawned on him—he had asked the oculus to show him Tala, but it had shown him Bliss instead. There had to be a connection between the girls. But what was it? Could Bliss lead him to Tala in some way? There had to be a reason for the oculus's answer.

It didn't help that when he looked at Bliss, it was as if his insides had turned to jelly. The oculus had masked the full effect of her beauty, and now that he didn't regard her as the enemy, he was unprepared for the reaction her presence stirred in him, and had even as he had meant to kill her in the butcher shop. Instant. Physical. Painful, even. He shook the feeling away; he had to ignore it. He wasn't that kind of wolf anymore.

"She is awake," Malcolm called from the backseat.

"Where are you taking me? Who are you guys? What

have you done with my aunt Jane? What the hell is going on?" she demanded.

"Lawson said you speak *Hroll*. This means you can't mean us any harm. He's sorry about what happened back at the shop. I'm Malcolm, by the way," Malcolm said sweetly. "And that's my brother. Lawson."

"Pleased to meet you both," Bliss said, her tone sarcastic. "Now why don't you tell me where you're taking me?"

Lawson caught her eye in the rear-view mirror. "I'd like to, but I need to know who you are first. I don't know what to make of you. I thought you were a tracker, but you speak our tongue, which means you aren't, but if you're not a spy, then what are you? But I'm getting ahead of myself. First things first: what do you know about Tala? Where is she?"

Bliss furrowed her brow. "Tala? I don't know who that is, I've never heard of her. I told you, I'm looking for my aunt Jane."

Lawson's heart sank. He'd had a feeling it wouldn't be as simple as he'd hoped, but there was still the possibility that Bliss could lead him to Tala, even if she didn't realize it herself. He just had to figure out how. He cleared his throat. "Next question, then—what are you? You're no ordinary mortal."

"I guess not. Seeing that I used to be a vampire," she snapped.

He hadn't expected her to say that. Malcolm yelped from the backseat.

"Easy there, Mac," Lawson said, looking back at Bliss. "You're one of the Fallen." He was not pleased. The Fallen were no friends to the wolves. They had left them to their fate, to their curse. The wolves had a role to play in their story, Arthur had told him, but Lawson wanted no part in it.

"I used to be. It's a long story." She looked away.

"I've got time."

"There was ... something wrong with me. I killed myself. Or at least I killed the vampire part of me. Whatever I was ... I'm not anymore. I'm just human now."

And she expected him to believe that? He wanted to laugh. "No one's just human. Especially not the Fallen."

"Maybe you're right," she said. "But that's my story."

"Not all of it," he said. "Why were you looking for us?"

Bliss paused, and Lawson wondered if that meant she was about to lie. "I wasn't looking for you exactly," she said finally. "Like I told you already, I was looking for my aunt Jane. She's missing, and I think ... the hounds have her."

"Hounds? Why do you think that?"

"From the way she was taken."

"And how was that?"

She described the room: everything torn up, as if raked by sharp claws, the whole place—bedspreads, curtains, sheets, pillows—shredded to pieces. "There was blood everywhere, and strange claw prints on the wall."

Lawson felt the hair on his arms rise as he listened to her tale. The hounds were afoot and had taken other victims, it sounded like. But why? Who was this Bliss Llewellyn and what was her connection to the hounds? Was he still right in thinking she would lead him to Tala somehow?

"My turn to ask questions now," she said. "What are *you*?"

"I'm a wolf," he said proudly. "We were once the *Abyssus Praetorium*."

"The Praetorian Guard," she whispered. "The guards of the abyss. The keepers of time, guardians of the passages."

"You know our history." He was pleased.

"Yes I do. Lucifer's dogs. The Hounds of Hell," she whispered, her face paling.

"Never call us by that name!" Lawson roared. The car veered to the side of the road and stopped abruptly.

Bliss was thrown against the front seat, and blood trickled from her forehead. She was shaking.

Lawson turned and glared at her. Malcolm cringed. "Lawson, please," his brother begged. "She doesn't know."

Bliss stared back at the two of them angrily. "Know what? Wolf, hound, all the same, isn't it?"

"No!" Lawson shook his head. "Never." He looked down at the steering wheel, at his white knuckles. "My brothers and I escaped from the pack a year ago, and we've been hiding and running ever since. We'll never be hounds, not if I can help it." He thought of Tala for a moment, wondered if those were empty words, remembered all his friends who were still left behind. "The masters turn wolf cubs into hellhounds on their eighteenth moon day. We had to run before we were turned."

"Right," Bliss said, and her tone of voice told him everything he needed to know. She didn't believe a word he'd said. That made two of them. Ex-vampire indeed. He gunned the engine and steered the car back to the road, and no one spoke until they reached the cave.

SIXTEEN

"Arthur says it's a show cave from the 1960s," the younger boy—Malcolm—was telling her. Bliss followed them out of the car and inside a dark cavern. She didn't see that she had a choice for now. She was their hostage, even if the older one—Lawson—didn't want to admit it. She only hoped he would take her to Jane; at least they would be together.

Bliss wasn't sure she believed his story about not being a hellhound. Even though she'd witnessed his wrath at being called such, she knew he'd meant to hurt her back at the butcher shop. *Hellhounds are uncontrollable, violent, and vicious*—yeah, he'd been all that.

Lawson. She hated him a little for being so strong— she was jealous, she supposed. She used to be a vampire, immortal, powerful; now she was just an ordinary girl with two broken legs. Bliss was annoyed with herself as well, for even noticing that he was attractive—handsome, with a strong jaw, a high forehead, and thick, dark hair. He was a killer—she'd seen it in his eyes. He was dangerous, brutal. She would have to watch her step around him—why had she told him so much about herself? Best not to reveal anything more, she decided.

The cavern was one long space that wound in an arc like the crescent of the moon, with a makeshift kitchen in the middle and a few scattered and dark utility rooms off to the side. Bliss followed Malcolm, who was still talking. "Arthur said back then they didn't care about preserving natural beauty, instead they put in linoleum and charged admission, whatever that means. But they've got some cool exhibits in the back."

"Who's Arthur?" she asked.

"He sort of . . . takes care of us—he moved here after the attack. Thought it would be safer if the hounds returned."

"The hounds? They attacked you too? Why?"

Bliss noticed Lawson giving his brother a hard look, and Malcolm grew quiet. She looked around at her new surroundings. The whole place smelled of mold and dust; it made her nose run and her eyes water. The cavern was cold and humid, like a basement with a broken steam pipe.

"We're back," Lawson called as they approached three figures sitting by the fire. "This is Bliss Llewellyn. We found her in the shop. That's Arthur," he said, pointing to an old gentleman in the corner, who smiled at her gently. "That's Rafe," he said, pointing to the stockier boy. "And that's Edon."

Bliss greeted them with a nod. None of them seemed to be surprised to see her. They must have known about the trap back at the butcher shop. She gazed at the four boys together. There was something savage and untamed about all of them, but something fierce and splendid as well. If Lawson was handsome, with the rugged good looks of a frontier cowboy, Edon was beautiful—his features were just a little finer, with an aristocratic cast, deep violet eyes and golden hair. Rafe was olive-skinned and almond-eyed; built like a rock, his body looked as if it could stop a Mack truck, but he had a sweet smile.

The boys were dressed appallingly. Their clothing was dirty, too small or too big, mismatched, and oddly chosen. Malcolm was wearing a yellow hooded sweatshirt, green corduroys, and pink Crocs. Rafe wore a flannel shirt and worn tuxedo pants. Edon, for all his hauteur and aloofness, was wearing a silly boy-band T-shirt and surfer shorts over long underwear. All their clothes were holey and worn, dirty and torn. Not even thrift stores would take them; they looked like things they had found in the garbage.

Rafe shook her hand while Edon appraised her coolly. "So this is the ex-vampire," Edon said. His voice was beautiful as well, smooth and melodic.

Bliss started—how could he know? The wolves must be able to communicate without speaking, she realized, able to use the glom just as the vampires did. "I like to think of myself more as newly human," she said, smiling thinly. "So you guys are wolves, are you? Escaped from Hell, Lawson says."

"Lawson says a lot of things," Edon said. "Why should we believe that you no longer have your fangs?"

"The same reason you want me to believe that you no longer do the work of the devil," Bliss retorted.

"We never did his work. We ran before we could do any harm. Do not speak of that of which you know nothing," Edon threatened, his voice a low and chilling growl.

"So what kind of name is Bliss?" Malcolm asked, changing the subject. "Is it a family name?"

"No." She shook her head. "The people who raised me weren't even my parents. Bliss isn't even my real name. At least, not where it matters. I found out that my real name is Lupus Theliel."

Malcolm gave her a curious look. "Lupus Theliel. Wolfsbane."

"Yes."

The younger boy exchanged looks with Lawson. "You must be part wolf, then . . . but you're one of the Fallen, which doesn't make sense," he said.

Bliss did not respond. There were things she couldn't tell them about herself yet, and the identity of her immortal father was one of them. She didn't know how they would react to hearing she was Lucifer's spawn, and wasn't sure she was ready to find out. "It's not much better than Bliss, but what are you going to do?"

"Change it," he replied. "Your name, I mean."

"Is that what you did?"

Malcolm raised an eyebrow.

"Your real name is Maccon, right?"

"How'd you know?"

"Because Maccon means 'wolf.' Just like Rafe. And Edon. You all have wolf names. Except for Lawson," she said, taking a seat as far away from his as possible.

Malcolm grinned. "I'd rather be called Lawson too if my name was Ulf."

Everyone laughed and Bliss found she could not

suppress a smile. Maybe they were telling the truth; maybe they weren't hounds after all. "So—what happens now? If you don't have Jane, and you aren't hellhounds, then why am I here?" she said, looking at Lawson in a challenging manner. "Because of some girl named Tala? I told you, I've never heard of anyone ..."

Lawson tossed her a piece of paper and she caught it in midair.

"What is this?" she asked, annoyed, looking at the picture in her hand. "*The Abduction of the Sabine Women*? What does that have to do with anything?" She glared at the postcard, which showed the famous painting by Nicolas Poussin that depicted a violent scene in history, of a group of women taken captive by Roman soldiers. They were throwing their arms into the air, calling for help or running in terror.

"Oh, sorry, wrong one," Lawson said, taking it back and handing her another picture. Then she saw that it was a photograph of a girl.

She was small, with a simple, narrow face, bright blue eyes, and pink streaks in her hair. Bliss thought she looked familiar—she had seen this girl before, but the hair was different—and with a dawning horror she realized it was the broken girl she had seen at the mental institution. "Lawson—" she said softly. "Is this Tala?"

Lawson was about to answer when Malcolm suddenly bent forward, clutching his stomach, and vomited violently all over the floor.

In a moment, the boys were standing, Arthur was mumbling incantations, and Lawson was barking orders.

"What's wrong? What's happening?" Bliss asked, feeling their panic.

"The hounds," Edon hissed. "They're here!"

SEVENTEEN

*T*here was a sound like the crack of a whip and Lawson collapsed to the ground, bleeding from a gaping wound on his side, the blood gushing in dark red bursts: a thick, viscous river.

"They got him with a blood spell!" Edon yelled as Rafe pushed Malcolm away, enveloping him in a hug and shielding his eyes.

"Don't look!" Rafe told the younger boy.

Arthur worked frantically, whispering as he waved his hands over the hole in Lawson's torso. Lawson's face was gray and he wasn't breathing, Bliss saw. She stood paralyzed until Rafe pulled at her hand. "Come on!" he yelled, leading her to the far end of the cavern. He was carrying Malcolm on his back.

She could hear muffled howls from far away and thought she saw shadows that weren't theirs flickering on the walls as they ran down the long stone ramp that circled through the cave. "Where are they?" she asked, her heart thudding in her chest.

"If they sent a blood spell, it means they were able to break down the wards," Rafe replied grimly. "They'll be inside soon."

"Damn Lawson to Hell," Edon said. "Romulus saw him in the oculus—he must have. Led them right to us."

"Lawson did?" Bliss asked. "But why?"

Edon ignored her question. "Or maybe it was you. Maybe you are a tracker after all."

She wanted to slap him.

"Stop it, Edon! Lawson said she spoke *Hroll*. She can't be one of them," Malcolm huffed.

Edon shut up and they ran in earnest. They were running so hard and fast that Bliss hunched momentarily from a leg cramp. She shook it off, irritated by her human limitations once more. When they reached the end of the curve, Rafe said a few words and the rock face opened on a hinge. A secret door led to a small tight corridor. "Can you see in the dark?" he asked.

"I don't know."

"Hold on, then," he said, and Bliss grabbed the tail of his T-shirt.

Behind them, she could hear Edon scrambling, and she heard Lawson scream—he wasn't dead yet—as Arthur performed his healing, and then heard an echo as a powerful force thundered against the cavern door, making the earth shake underneath their feet. Her heart was beating a million times a minute.

"Don't worry, they won't be able to get in, not that way, at least," Rafe said as there was the sound of another hard thud, and the ground rumbled again. It felt as if the whole cavern was on the verge of collapse.

"Can they pass through stone?" she asked as they scrambled forward in the dark, the passage sloping downward.

"Yes. But it'll slow them down. Hold on to this side," he said. "Or you'll fall off the cliff."

"What about Lawson?" she asked, wondering why she cared so much about a boy who'd just tried to kill her. She barely knew him, barely knew any of them. And if the hounds were here, shouldn't she be running toward them instead of away?

"I don't know," Rafe said, his voice tight. "He's never been like this. He always heals so fast, always."

They kept running for what felt like miles, and there was a sound of clattering footsteps behind them.

Malcolm whooped when they saw that Lawson was bringing up the rear. He still looked pale, but through the hole in his shirt she could see that his skin was smooth and the blood had dried.

"It wasn't a blood spell. It just felt like it was. It was just an exploder," he explained, leaning on Arthur, who was holding a torch and looking grim. "But they broke those wards like they were made of glass."

"They've gotten stronger," Arthur said. "How unfortunate."

"You didn't feel them coming, Mac?" Lawson asked.

"Not soon enough. Not until it was too late." Malcolm shook his head, looking ashamed.

Malcolm was about to apologize again when Lawson clamped a hand on his mouth. "Shhh!" No one dared to speak. Bliss watched Lawson. He was counting. She swallowed and held her breath. The room was so still they were frozen. She was conscious of her own pulse, the air around her face, and the temperature of the cave.

"Four heartbeats," Lawson whispered. "Inside. Two in the scullery now, the others somewhere around the dioramas."

Edon nodded. "Sounds about right. I can't feel any more."

"Reconnaissance team, most likely," Lawson said. "Hurry. We can outrun them."

"Why can't we jump?" Malcolm asked. "Make the circle?"

"You know why." Lawson shook his head. "I can't take that risk again, not when there's so little time." He had taken a few steps forward when he turned around and froze. His brothers did the same; the four boys stood with their noses in the air, sniffing like dogs.

"They've found us," Malcolm said, shaking a little.

"We can take them," Lawson said. "Arthur—take Mac and Bliss down to the car. Don't wait. We'll meet you at the rendezvous point."

He turned to Bliss, held her arm. "Don't let them touch you," he warned. "Otherwise you'll be dragged down to Hell with them."

Then Bliss heard the three older boys chanting under their breath and saw a blue crescent appear on their faces; Lawson's throbbed above his right cheekbone.

But before they were done, the hellhounds came out of the walls, howling for blood.

rthur fell first. His knee bent at an unnatural angle and he reeled sideways. His torch fell to the ground, still flickering. He moaned and tried to stand, but a dark shadow hit him on the jaw and he doubled over on the ground.

Lawson was on him in a flash, drawing the hound away. *Come out!* he yelled. *Stop hiding in the dark, cowards!*

All his fault. Edon was right. Romulus had recognized him, of course, and had pinpointed his location; it hadn't taken them that long once the hounds found the right scent. Or was it Bliss who had led them here? He'd heard Edon accuse her as well. Had she led the hounds to them? He was confused and angry, but there was no time to dwell on mistakes just then.

Draw them out of the glom, he thought, out of the shadow, where they will have to fight hand to hand. He leapt at the hound but caught nothing but air.

He could hear his brothers doing the same dance, swinging at shadows, fighting phantoms, chasing after specters, Rafe grunting, Edon cursing, while the hounds surrounded them. The biggest one came straight for Lawson, but Lawson saw him coming and feinted left, then struck, holding the hound in a choke hold.

Where's Tala? he demanded. *Where is she? What did you do to her?*

The hound smiled a cruel smile. *The little one? She's dead, of course. We killed her. But first we made her scream. We made her beg for death at the end. Death was kind after what we did to her. You did this. You killed her. You left her to die. You left her to burn.*

Return to us. Take the whip. The mantle is yours. Romulus will forgive. Bring us your brothers.

"NO!" Lawson cried, falling back and releasing the hound. They both fell into the glom, where Lawson's rage transformed him into a wolf. They were all wolves now, Rafe large and black-furred and red-eyed, Edon golden and lean, his teeth sharp as razors—wolves with red markings around their necks, where their collars had once choked them.

Lawson snarled at the hounds that surrounded them;

they had transformed as well, shedding their human aspect for bestial form, with sleek glossy hides, sharp ivory teeth, and long silver claws. He leapt at the nearest one, his teeth bared, seeking blood. Blood and revenge.

He made quick work of the beasts, breaking the necks of two, smashing the third against the wall. Four. Only one left.

Where? he sent.

Rafe shook his head. Edon paced the stone. *It got away.*

Then he saw it—it was running toward the light, toward the end of the passage, running for the girl. Bliss. Arthur and Malcolm were far ahead, almost at the end. But Bliss was slow—not a vampire anymore, she'd told him. Lawson snarled, bared his teeth, and ran as fast as he could.

Bliss had fallen and her leg was bleeding. She was cringing away from the hound—Lawson could see its shape as it loomed large above her, casting a huge shadow. Its crimson eyes were brilliant with hatred.

He roared at the hound, and the monster turned to him.

The hellhound growled and leapt to attack, its claws tearing into Lawson's body, from neck to stomach; then it sunk its teeth into Lawson's neck and began to shake him like a rag doll.

"REVERTO UT ABYSSUS! REVERTO UT OBSCU-RUM!"

Lawson turned to see Bliss holding aloft the knife from the butcher shop. Her eyes were blazing, her voice ringing with the tone of command. He held his breath, waiting for the hound to mount another attack—a human girl with a kitchen knife as her only weapon was no match for a hound of Hell—but instead the beast cringed before Bliss, yelping and turning tail, whining as it retreated, disappearing into the night.

He turned back into his human form, and Bliss helped him to his feet. He was bleeding from the cuts in his neck, on his torso. "Who are you, Bliss Llewellyn?" he asked weakly. "The hound feared you."

There was a heavy silence, broken by another pop— Rafe and Edon appeared, as humans. Both were bleeding from cuts and breathing heavily.

"Where's the hound?" Rafe asked, spitting out a tooth.

"It left," Lawson said. "Bliss told it to go away."

Edon scratched his head. "Curious." The boys all looked at her then, fear and suspicion in their eyes.

PART THREE

I change shapes just to hide in this place
But I'm still, I'm still an animal.

Mike Snow, "Animal"

NINETEEN

"She spoke the sacred language," Lawson said. "I didn't recognize it at first, it had been so long since I'd heard the language of the masters."

"You seem to have a great talent for languages," Edon said drily.

Bliss shrugged and tossed away the knife, dark with the hound's blood. She wasn't going to answer their questions.

They stood in a tense circle until Arthur came out of the darkness. The old man was breathing heavily, and he had a cut on his forehead where the hound had hit him, but he was all right. He nodded at the group. "You got them all? Good." He nodded to Lawson. "We'll have to do something about that wound or you'll bleed out," he said, motioning to the gaping wound in Lawson's belly.

"It's not that bad," Lawson said.

Bliss grimaced, noticing for the first time the Swiss-cheese pattern of wounds that littered his torso. His shirt was steeped in blood.

Lawson began to protest, but Arthur would hear none of it. "Malcolm, collect the healing ointments. Rafe, Edon, reinforce the wards around the cave." The boys left for their tasks.

"What do you need, Arthur?" Bliss asked.

"Help me get his clothes off first. I'll get some warm compresses," Arthur said, leaving them together.

"You don't have to stay," Lawson said. "I can take off my own clothes."

"It's fine," Bliss said. "Nothing I haven't seen before," she snapped.

"You might be surprised," he said.

She pulled off his shirt a little roughly, and the fabric scraped the open wounds.

"Ouch!" he yelped before he could help himself.

"Sorry," she said. She struggled to conceal the horror on her face when she saw the extent of his injuries, continuing to undress him until he was naked underneath a cool sheet to cover the terrifying sight of broken bone and skin and muscle, the blood congealed into a purple cake.

Arthur came back and lifted the sheet, examining the wounds. He nodded, muttered a few things to himself, and then put the sheet back down. "Clean him up as well as you can," he told Bliss. "I'll need to collect a few other things before we begin."

"You gonna make it through this?" Lawson asked, challenging her.

"I'll be fine," she said, but her voice was gentler. She cleaned his face first, dabbing slowly at the crusted blood and pus, wiping the dirt away. Bliss felt his eyes on her as she cleaned the rag, submerging it in the warm water and removing it, rolling it into a tube and wringing it out before returning it to his skin. Soon the pan of water was red with blood. Her hand was shaking a little as she cleaned around the wounds.

"It's okay," he said. "It doesn't hurt that much."

"Liar," she said softly.

Arthur returned. "Lawson, it's time."

"What?" Bliss asked, pausing with the wet rag in the air and looking between Arthur and Lawson, whose face had turned even paler.

"I'm going to burn it out," Arthur said, confirming

his fear. "To leach the poison. I'm sorry, Lawson, but it can't be helped. It's the only way."

"Do your worst," he said, sucking air through his teeth.

"You're going to burn him?" Bliss asked.

"Hellhound claws are poisoned with silver, which is slowly dissolving into his blood, to keep the wounds fresh, to make sure they never heal. We're going to have to burn it from his blood. You might not want to see this."

"*I* don't want to see this," Lawson said.

Bliss shook her head, with no hesitation. "I'm not afraid of blood."

"Are you sure?" Arthur asked.

She rolled up her sleeves, a determined look on her face. "You're going to need someone to help hold him down."

The fire made a sizzling sound as it hit the silver, and Lawson shook and fought and kicked and screamed in agony, but Bliss kept his arms above his head, holding him until her palms were red and sweaty, fighting him, so that Arthur could do his job. She found Lawson's casual disregard for his own safety appalling and heroic at the same time. "It's working," she said, watching each wound close and the skin turn smooth as the fire burned out.

Lawson's face contorted in pain, but he finally

stopped struggling and his wrists went slack. By the end of it her clothing was muddy with his blood and the room smelled like smoke. Arthur put his tools away. "That should take care of it," he said, leaving the two of them alone.

Lawson turned to Bliss. "Thank you," he croaked. "I know that wasn't pretty."

She tossed him his shirt and pants and looked away while he got dressed. She felt closer to him after the experience; she had seen the depths of his suffering, and she was somehow no longer afraid of him. This was a boy she could count on, she thought, someone who was strong, who could bear a burden without flinching or weakening.

"So you're going to tell me what happened back there? How you got that hound to leave us alone?" Lawson asked.

"I don't know." It was a weak answer, and she could tell he wasn't buying it. But she couldn't afford to tell him the truth. Not yet. She could still feel the hound's dank breath on her. She had looked straight into its crimson eyes, sure that death was upon her, and it had turned away. *Who are you, Bliss Llewellyn? The hound feared you.*

There was only one reason the hellhound had left them alone: it had taken her for its master. *Lucifer's dogs.*

And she was Lucifer's daughter. She might have killed the spirit of her father inside her, but she was still his flesh and blood. The hound knew what she was. The hound knew she was one of them.

If Lawson knew, if any one of them knew … She knew she could never tell them. They could never know the truth about her. Lawson would kill her without question this time. She had seen what he did to hellhounds. She had seen his mouth red with the blood of the hounds he had slain.

"You don't know," Lawson repeated. "Tell me the truth—this didn't start with your aunt's kidnapping, did it?"

"No." Bliss shook her head. Maybe even if she couldn't tell him about her father, it was time to come clean about something else. "Meeting you wasn't a co-incidence. You were partly right … I was looking for wolves, but not for Romulus." She bit her lip. "There's a war going on among us … with the Silver Bloods … the same demons who are your former masters … and my people are losing. I was sent to find the wolves, to help us. My mother told me that the wolves were demon fighters and that we will need your help in order to win the war against Lucifer. I'm supposed to bring your kind back to them … to join the fight."

"And why should we do that?" Lawson asked. So this was the part the wolves were to play, he realized; this was what Arthur had been preparing him for.

"I don't know. I was sort of hoping you would know. My mother—she was the one who set this all up, but she didn't tell me very much except that I had to find you."

Lawson crinkled his forehead. "Arthur said a friend of his told him to help us . . . he called her Gabrielle."

"Lawson—Gabrielle is—Gabrielle of the Angels. Allegra Van Alen. She's my mother."

He stared at her. "You are an archangel's daughter."

"In our history books, in our repository, it says the hounds turned against their masters once," Bliss said.

"Yes. But we paid for it dearly. Lucifer punished the wolves for their disobedience. We were cast into the hellfire, and he turned us into little more than animals." Lawson looked grim and troubled. "We were once the Praetorian Guard, keepers of the passages, but now . . . we are nothing but a bunch of fighting dogs."

Bliss shook her head. "I don't believe in the permanence of curses," she said. "Otherwise . . . I would have given up long ago." She shuddered. "What does Romulus have to do with any of this? I've heard of him, but not in connection with our history."

"He was one of us, he was our leader, but he betrayed

us, sold us to the demons, for power, to curry Lucifer's favor," Lawson said.

Bliss scratched her nose. "Yikes."

"Yep."

"Can I ask you something?" she said.

"Anything." He smiled and Bliss smiled back. They looked at each other for a long time, but finally, she broke away from his intense gaze.

"Your . . . brothers . . . you guys don't look alike."

"You noticed."

"Well . . . " Bliss laughed.

"We're not brothers in the usual sense," he said. "We don't have the same parents. Wolves don't even know their parents. We're taken from our mothers as soon as we're whelped. But we are brothers. We made a pact to each other. It's like the opposite of the curse."

"The anti-curse." Bliss smiled. She liked the sound of that. "Lawson, the girl in the picture—the attack Malcolm mentioned—the hounds took Tala, didn't they?"

"Yes."

"And she was special to you."

"Yes."

Bliss wrung the edge of her shirt. "I understand. Even before the hounds took Aunt Jane, I lost someone too."

His name was Dylan Ward, she thought. She had loved him at first sight, that first night at the club when everything had happened, when her life had changed. She could still see his dark hair and dark eyes illuminated by the flame he'd held out to her. It felt so long ago. *Dylan,* she thought, and she felt the tears well up in her eyes again. *I miss you.* He had been her rock and her escape through that long terrible year when she had been a prisoner in her own mind. He had helped her and she had freed him. She had loved him with all her heart and soul, but he was gone now.

"He won't return?" Lawson asked quietly.

"No. He's gone. He's somewhere else now, a better place." Bliss looked down at her empty hands. "I have to let go."

Lawson took her hand in his. "I can't. I know Tala is out there. I know I can find her. I know I can save her."

"Yes, you can," Bliss said, her eyes shining. "Because I know where she is."

TWENTY

*A*rthur Beauchamp insisted on staying behind. The four boys and Bliss were packed into his beat-up van. The old warlock looked frail but resolute in front of his cavern. The woods were quiet and all was still in the middle of the night, with no sign of the battle that had raged.

Lawson felt his wounds healing underneath his bandages, but his chest hurt for a different reason. He remembered seeing the old man at the park bench a year earlier. How scared they had been, and how relieved to find help at last, shelter, education, guidance. Arthur had been more than their guardian, he was a friend. "Come with us," he said again.

"No, my boy, when they realize what happened, the

hounds will return in greater numbers. I will hold them here for as long as I am able," Arthur said. "Besides, I am not without reinforcements." He removed a wand from his suit pocket. It was ebony and made of bone. Dragon bone, the warlock had explained to them once. An ancient magic, older than the underworld, made before the earth was formed. It shone in the dim light, gleaming with sparks. "I think it is time I broke my restriction."

"Arthur—I can't ask you to do this," Lawson said.

"*You* did not ask me. Someone else did," Arthur said with a wry smile. He turned to Bliss. "I owe your mother a favor. Yes, I saw the resemblance. You have her eyes." He held up the wand, making an arc in the air. "I failed her once, long ago. In Florence, when she needed a friend. I told her I would make up for it—I told her to ask me anything, and I would do it. This was my promise. That I would keep you boys safe, and I will."

"Goodbye, Arthur," Bliss said. "Lawson—we should go."

Lawson revved the engine. Malcolm waved. Edon and Rafe nodded their goodbyes.

Arthur waved his white handkerchief. "With luck, we shall cross paths again one day. Lawson, don't forget what I told you about the passages. Now leave me to it."

*

The hospital wasn't far. Lawson couldn't believe Tala had been so close. He should never have left her. Was it truly this easy? Were his dreams to be fulfilled that night?

"This is it," Bliss said when they arrived at the four-story building at the top of the hill. Lawson let the van idle in the parking lot as he staked out the place. The hospital was dark, the lobby closed for the night, curtains drawn. There was a sleepy guard at the front entrance who didn't seem to notice the van parked at the far end of the lot.

Lawson turned off the engine. "Rafe, Mac, you guys stay here. Edon, come with me." It would be safer if it was just a small team, and he and Edon could handle whatever came up. He was leading them toward the back entrance when he stopped.

"What is it?" Edon whispered.

Lawson pointed to the bronze cross emblazoned on the hospital doors, and the name of the clinic: St. Bernadette's Psychiatric Clinic. His heart began to beat wildly in his chest, bursting with hope. If Tala was alive and unharmed, if she'd managed to escape the hounds, she would have sought refuge in a place like this—a holy place that the hounds could never enter. A place she would be safe.

"Crap," Edon swore.

"What's with him?" asked Bliss.

"Oh nothing, he's just a little irked he can't go inside," Lawson explained.

"St. Bernadette's?" Bliss asked.

"Hallowed ground," Lawson explained. "Off-limits to underworld scum."

"I'll wait outside," Edon said. "Take it easy in there. We've had enough fireworks for the day."

"How come *you* can come in?" Bliss asked as Lawson jiggered the back door open.

"Dunno. I just can. Discovered it by accident one day at a church soup kitchen. Rest of the boys couldn't cross the threshold, but I snuck in smooth as butter. Maybe someone likes me up there," he said as he pushed the door open, and then they were inside. "I cut the alarm, don't worry." He stopped at the foot of the stairs. "You remember where she was?"

"Room fifteen. I think it was on the third floor."

It wasn't. The hospital was a maze of identical hallways and rooms, and to make matters more confusing, there were several room fifteens. None of them held Tala. There was a nurses' station at each landing, but they managed to move around without being noticed.

"I'm sorry—everything looks the same. This is the

hospital, though. Maybe they moved her," Bliss said as she looked around nervously.

He followed her down a corridor that led away from the main part of the hospital. "This is it!" she said excitedly as they came upon a room with a guard's stool in front of it, but there was no guard. And when Lawson opened the door, the room was empty. But he sensed a presence that felt strange and familiar at the same time. *Tala?*

"This was the room, right?" he asked.

"I think so," Bliss replied.

This isn't right. It isn't the right scent. But maybe it has been too long . . . maybe being with the hounds has changed her . . . He couldn't breathe. There was too much to hope for, too much at stake.

"What is it? What's wrong?"

"I'm not sure . . . " He paced the room one more time and then turned to Bliss. "Follow me."

He banged the door open and darted down the hallway, brushing past a nurse so quickly that she dropped her tray. "Sorry!"

"Hey! You can't be in here!" the nurse yelled, but he was already at the stairs. He turned back to make sure Bliss was following him. *Down. She's down the stairs. To the right.*

He caught the scent again from a ventilation duct and tracked it down a long hallway, then stopped at the farthest door. "In here," he said. He put his hand on the doorknob. It wasn't locked. He walked inside.

There was a girl on the bed. She was hooked to a drip line and sleeping quietly. Lawson walked to her side and stared down at the sleeping girl. Her hair looked different; her skin was so pale it was translucent; she looked half-dead. *What have they done to you?*

Next to him, Bliss read the label on the bag of fluid attached to the girl's arm. "She's heavily sedated. Probably why there's no guard anymore, no need for locks."

Of course not, Lawson thought. No need for locks, not with that industrial-strength dope they're feeding her. She must have really scared the life out of everyone to earn that much of a dose.

He felt Bliss put a hand on his shoulder. "It's okay," she said. "Tala's going to be all right, we're going to get her out of here." He shook his head and he gripped the metal bars on the bed so tightly his knuckles were white.

"Lawson . . . what's the matter?"

The girl opened her eyes then. Her bright blue eyes were the color of the sky, but her voice was mocking. "I think he's expecting someone else," she said.

"Ahramin," he said. The girl in the bed was the hound who'd been at their doorstep, the same girl who had bested him for alpha.

The day of the trials, when the gates had lifted, he had expected to see Varg, his strongest opponent. Instead, a lithe figure emerged from the shadows. Ahramin. He'd stared at her, unbelieving, but there was no sympathy in her eyes. She had fought him ferociously and she had triumphed. She had sunk her teeth into his neck. Had lifted him by the hair, displayed his white throat to Romulus, would have torn it, slashed it with her teeth, from ear to ear, but the general had spared him, and Lawson had been able to live.

But Tala was right, Lawson thought. *I let her win.* The masters had thrown him for a loop. He could not kill her—not Ahramin, one of his own, one from his den. He had been caught off guard and been defeated. He had allowed Ahramin to live, thinking he had made the bigger sacrifice. He had been prepared to meet his death rather than take her life. How could he have foreseen that doing so would mean that one day she would unleash the forces of Hell on his pack and destroy the only home he had ever known?

TWENTY-ONE

"Who's Ahramin?" Bliss asked.

"Tell her, Lawson. Tell her who I am. That's what they call you now, is it? Lawson? Strange name. But then again, you were always a little different," Ahramin said. "Nice to see you again, sorry about that house. It looked . . . cozy."

Lawson clenched his jaw. He ignored her and answered Bliss. "She was one of us. Tala's sister. But they caught her when we escaped from Hell . . . "

"And they turned me into one of them." Ahramin looked at Bliss. "Hello again. So you found wolves instead of hounds, did you? Interesting. I wondered if you would return."

Bliss thought Ahramin did look like Tala; she had the

same almond-shaped blue eyes and the same fair skin, the same long face, the same slight build. But she didn't have Tala's round cheeks and a pretty smile. Ahri was taut, lean, and tense. She was like a lioness ready to spring. Dangerous. Untrustworthy.

"You're a hellhound," Bliss breathed. She should have known from the beginning, thinking of the dread that surrounded the room, the strange things that had happened to the nurses, the janitors.

"Not quite." Ahramin's face crumpled and for a brief moment Bliss saw the broken girl from the other day. "You've got to believe me, Lawson, I'm not a hound anymore. I'm not anything. Not even a wolf. I can't shift. I can't do anything. When I failed to bring you to him, Romulus broke my collar." She pulled her gown lower to show them the jagged black line around her neck, an imprint of the collar that used to be there. "He left me in that house to die, left me for dead in that fire we set for you."

"She's a hellhound, Lawson," Bliss warned. "She might have been your friend once but she's not anymore."

"You can't leave me here!" Ahramin cried. "You would abandon me again after everything?" she said, challenging him. "After my sacrifice?"

"Lawson—!" Bliss said, watching with horror as Lawson moved toward Ahramin and began to untie her foot restraints. "Think about it! You said so yourself— there's no going back after the change. You don't know what she's capable of!"

But Lawson ignored her, although Ahramin didn't seem to need any help—she ripped off the needles and wrenched her wrists out of their plastic shackles seemingly without effort. She nodded a thank-you to Lawson and walked out of the room, holding her hospital gown tightly closed. She walked regally, with her head held high, like a queen, the cheap cotton fabric like armor or couture. "Which way?" she asked when they came to the hallway.

"Here," Lawson said, leading them up the back staircase. He seemed cowed somehow, okay with taking orders. Bliss didn't know what to make of it. Maybe he was shell-shocked; maybe he was doing it only out of guilt. But there seemed to be no talking him out of it.

A nurse tried to stop them and Ahramin merely smirked. "I'm taking a walk."

If it was so easy to walk out, why hadn't she done it before? Bliss wondered. Why stay here? Because it was the only place she was safe from the hounds, Lawson had explained. Hallowed ground. Blessed space. *Off-limits to underworld scum.* There was no way Ahramin could still be a hellhound if she was allowed into St. Bernadette's. Maybe that was why Lawson was so confident that she was on their side? Bliss hoped so.

When they exited the hospital, Ahramin stopped in her tracks. Edon, startled by the noise, turned around and looked right at her. He gaped at her. "Ahri . . . Oh my god . . . Ahri . . . "

Ahramin blinked her eyes. Edon hesitantly moved closer to her, a half smile forming on his lips. But the smile disappeared when he saw the hard, closed look on her face.

"Ahri—I'm so sorry—we failed you."

"Save your apologies, Edon," Ahramin said, her voice cold and flat. "I have no need to hear them."

Edon froze, his entire face red, as if she had just slapped him, and Bliss realized that somehow—without raising a hand—Ahramin had. Whatever had gone on between Edon and Ahramin was over; that much was clear.

"How are we getting out of here?" Ahramin asked.

"I'll get the van," Lawson said. Edon remained frozen, a statue, stricken, lost. "You guys, wait here."

"I'll come with you," Bliss said hurriedly. She ran to catch up with Lawson. "What's the deal, Lawson? Why'd you let her out of there—you don't know if she's telling the truth. Are you sure you're doing the right thing?"

"I can't abandon her. Back in the underworld, she was the head of our pack," he replied. "She bested me at the trials. She was our alpha."

"Well, alpha dog or not," Bliss said, "she's a real bitch."

Ahramin was kinder and softer upon being reunited with Rafe and Malcolm. She ruffled the younger boy's hair and smiled at Rafe. They piled back into the van and decided to drive to find the nearest campsite, Bliss in the back between Edon and Ahramin, who barely said a word to each other, Lawson and Rafe up front, with Malcolm in between, while Rafe drove.

"How did you guys end up hanging out with a vampire?" Ahramin asked, lighting a cigarette and rolling down her window. "You do know that's what she is, don't you?"

"I'm human," Bliss said with an edge to her voice. Where had Ahramin even found a pack of smokes? She'd walked out of the hospital in nothing but a cotton gown, but somehow she'd commandeered Edon's leather jacket and found his secret habit. Bliss frowned. She'd seen girls like Ahramin before, knew what they were like. She wasn't going to let her push her around, alpha or not. "You don't know anything about me."

"Bliss was the one who led us to you—without her,

we'd never have found you," Lawson said, his voice firm. "You owe her."

"If you say so." Ahramin shrugged, then coughed noisily.

"How did you survive?" Lawson asked Ahramin, turning around to address her directly. "We all know what happens to a hound without a collar."

"What happens?" Bliss wanted to know.

"They die," Ahramin replied cheerfully. "It's pretty gruesome. The collars become part of a hound's soul, so when they rip it off, it's like ripping your heart out."

"Why are you here, then?" Bliss asked sharply.

"Maybe it's because I held on to a little part of myself, even after the change," Ahramin said quietly. "All I know is that when I woke up, I wasn't dead. Losing a collar would have killed a hound, but maybe it's because I was never completely a hound. When they turned me, I fought the transformation as hard as I could—and I think that somehow, I was able to hang on to a little bit of my soul. Of course, when the mortals found me, the Red Bloods sent me to the nuthouse. They said I was insane and maybe I did go out of my mind a little after everything that happened." She coughed again, a raspy, horrible choking noise.

"Quite a story, it seems awfully convenient," Bliss said. "That there's no going back except for you ... "

"I believe you," Lawson interrupted.

What was he doing? Bliss wanted to punch him. He accepted Ahramin without question—it was maddening. She didn't understand him, and felt a twinge of jealousy. He'd wanted to kill her, but with Ahramin—this *hellhound*—he was as cowed as a puppy.

"But you want to know about Tala," Ahramin said coolly.

"Yes." The air in the van was tense, and the smoke didn't help.

Bliss could tell how difficult it was for Lawson to hold it together. He'd been filled with hope on the drive to the hospital, and now his hope had been dashed on the rocks. Steady now, she thought. Steady.

"Before I tell you what happened to my sister, first let me tell you what the transformation was like," Ahramin said. "No one ever tells you what really happens in the pen. When they turn us into hounds. They strip you down. Not just to the skin, but to the soul. They make you forget—everything. They plunge the collar into your body, so that the silver leaches inside, becomes part of your blood. It's why all the hounds have silver eyes with crimson pupils. The poison becomes part of your body. You become the poison."

Edon made a strangled noise and tried to reach across

Bliss to put a hand on Ahramin's arm but she shrugged it off impatiently, as if to show she didn't need any consolation.

"Then you hear it—all the time—Romulus's voice, in your head. In your dreams. He becomes part of you. It's . . . inescapable. Do you know what it's like, being a slave to someone else's will?"

"Yes," Bliss said curtly, thinking of the way Lucifer had used her. "I do."

Ahramin ignored her. "They didn't make me come for you in the beginning. In the beginning I was just another drone. Another hound on a leash. Finally, they said it was time. They wanted to know how we had done it, and where they could find you. They'd tried without me, of course, but had been unsuccessful. Now they wanted my help. I had to track you down, bring you back, or Romulus would have my collar. For a while, like I said, I still remembered enough of my life that I was able to resist them at first."

She tossed her cigarette out the window and lit another. "But I had to give in at the last. It was too painful. You know what they do, you know what they're like. I had no choice. I agreed to lead them to you. We looked for you everywhere. Finally I got the scent. You stayed too long in one place."

"Tala . . . I need to know what happened to Tala . . ." Lawson interrupted.

But Ahramin continued her monologue. "So she did become your mate. I thought that might happen after she escaped with you. Still, she was such a plain little thing . . . you never even noticed her before. You never cared for her in the underworld."

"What happened to her, Ahramin? What did they do to her?"

"They did what you might imagine." She shrugged. As if it were nothing. But her eyes were shining with tears.

Bliss could see Lawson's shoulders slump in the front seat. She glared at the dark-haired girl sitting next to her. "Stop torturing him. Answer the question. What happened to her?"

"Is she dead? Is Tala dead?" Lawson asked, his voice a hoarse whisper.

"No." Ahramin blew another smoke ring. It lingered in the air above them before dissipating, filling the van with its acrid smell. "But she may as well be. She's with Romulus now."

TWENTY-TWO

*B*liss offered to pay for a hotel. After everything that had happened, everything they had learned, it seemed like a small consolation but a necessary one. No one had spoken in the van after Ahramin's announcement; Lawson had completely broken down, his face turning gray and blank, as if he had been shot, as if he were dead already. Bliss took command then—someone had to; Edon was just as useless as Lawson after Ahramin's rejection, and Rafe and Malcolm looked too frightened to know what to do. She ushered the boys into their own room and placed Ahramin in hers. The "former" hellhound—Bliss still had her doubts—seemed a bit subdued by the reaction to her news and had barely said a word to Bliss before bedding down.

A few hours later, unable to sleep, Bliss crept out of the room, thinking she would take a walk in the hotel lobby to try to find something to distract her from her thoughts. Was it just two days earlier that she had been with Aunt Jane? How was it possible that so much had changed—meeting the boys, the attack by the hounds, looking for Tala and finding Ahramin instead? Bliss wasn't even sure what would happen next. She had to find a way to the hounds to find her aunt, of course; that was clear. But the boys—Lawson—what would happen to them—to him? Would he consent to doing as she asked? Would he consent to taking his pack to the vampires and fighting for them?

It was hours after midnight and the floor was deserted. Not even the front desk was staffed; there was only a bell to ring if you needed someone. Her footsteps echoed in the hallway. The lobby was standard-issue mid-range hotel, with a fireplace in the middle and comfortable armchairs and couches arrayed around it. She walked closer to the smoldering fire.

"Can't sleep either?" a voice asked.

She turned to find Lawson slouched down on a couch, an empty six-pack by his side. He was drinking from an open bottle of vodka.

"You planning on drinking that whole thing?" she asked.

"Only if you help me," he said. He was so obviously tipsy, slurring his words, his eyes bloodshot. But somehow, with his dark hair falling into his eyes, he still looked unbelievably sexy.

"Lawson—"

"Come on. I have chasers somewhere. That's what they're called, right? Chasers? To chase away the taste of alcohol. Although why anyone would want to do that, I don't know. Anyway, there's a box of orange juice ..." He waved feebly around the area.

Bliss took a seat next to him. Getting drunk was no way to react—but how could one react to such news, anyway? His pain was etched all over his face. He looked like a ghost, all the vitality and life drained from his face, his sorrow and grief manifested in his hunching walk, his hooded eyes. She reached for the vodka bottle and took a big gulp.

"That's my girl," he said, clapping her shoulder.

"Whoa," she said, feeling a bit dizzy. Alcohol had had no effect on her before; she kept forgetting she was human now. She put down the bottle and turned to him. "Maybe there's still hope—"

"There's not," he said, cutting her off. "Romulus will never let her go. Now that he knows what she means to me." He grabbed the bottle and took a swig. "I put her

166

in danger ... I never should have left her. It's all my fault."

"You didn't have a choice, and she wanted you to go, to survive," she said, reminding him of what he'd told her about that fateful night. She took the vodka away from him.

Lawson shook his head. "I'm selfish ... I went to the oculus ... the hounds could have killed us all tonight ... and ... and ... " He began to hiccup and fell forward into her arms, his whole body shaking. "I failed her. I practically gave her to him ... who knows what he's done to her ... killed her ... maybe he turned her into a hound early ... maybe she died from the change ... "

"I'm so sorry," Bliss whispered. "I'm so sorry." She held him to her chest, put her arms around him, felt his tears soak her robe. It hurt her to see him like this, so destroyed. "I'm so sorry, you don't deserve this," she said, and without thinking she began to kiss his head, his hair. She just wanted to make him feel better somehow, to erase, and to bear, some of his pain.

Lawson put his arms around her back and drew her closer, and then they were kissing, and his tears fell on her face, but he was kissing her, so passionately, as if he had been awoken, inspired, and she was kissing him back, as fiercely as he was kissing her. And his hands were slipping

Melissa de la Cruz

off her robe and she was melting into him, slipping his shirt over his head, and her palms were on his abdomen, his sculpted stomach . . .

And still he was kissing her, kissing her neck and groaning against her. He had stopped crying, she noticed . . . and neither of them was thinking of Ahramin or Tala or anyone else. He began to unbutton her shirt while she tugged at the button on his jeans. He loomed over her, and he looked at her, truly looked at her, his golden eyes fixed on hers, and she realized he was not drunk in the least and neither was she; they were both completely sober, and they both wanted this, wanted each other, so much.

She pulled him toward her, pulled him closer, to feel his warmth and his strength, and she wanted him . . . she wanted this to happen . . . but . . .

"Wait," she said. "Wait."

Not like this, she thought. Not like this. It would be too easy to discount it, too easy to pretend it was just a mistake, just an accident, just a hookup. Because he'd just found out about Tala, because they'd been drinking. She liked him too much for that.

"Wait," she said.

He fell against her, his body crashing on hers, and rested his head in the crook of her neck. She could feel

him breathing against her skin—hard, ragged breaths—
as the warmth between them began to cool.

"You're right," he said. "I'm sorry . . . I didn't mean
to . . ."

Then he said no more. He pulled away from her and
then he was gone, without another word, without a look
back, and even though it had been her idea to stop, Bliss
was the one who felt bereft, alone, seated in front of the
fireplace, its ashes long gone cold. It was freezing in the
room; she hadn't noticed. Lawson's body was so warm.

He had disappeared so quickly that for a moment she
was uncertain whether anything had truly happened
between them, or whether it had just been a dream.

TWENTY-THREE

The next morning the group convened at the van, sipping cups of lukewarm coffee and munching on free doughnuts from the hotel buffet. Bliss nodded to Lawson, who nodded back, tipping his cup toward her. She was determined to put it all behind them and to forget about what had happened the night before. They'd both been really drunk, right? That was all it was. From the way he was acting, it looked as if he felt the same way.

Part of her was annoyed at that, wanted some sort of sign from him that the previous night had mattered—even a little—that he hadn't just blocked it from his memory.

Then again, what did she really want from him, anyway? A relationship? It was too soon for both of them; she saw that now. Plus, what would happen if he found out who she really was? It was better just to forget about the whole thing. They'd made a mistake getting too close.

Earlier that morning she had bought them all a change of clothes at the gift shop, and of course Ahramin still looked good even in a silly tourist T-shirt and shorts. She was holding court in the middle of the group, the boys hanging on to her every word.

"What's going on?" Bliss whispered, sliding next to Malcolm. Ahramin and Lawson seemed to be in the middle of an argument.

"Ahramin has news," Malcolm said. "But Lawson's not sure if he believes her."

"What kind of news?"

"You said you knew about the Praetorian Guard?"

"A little, yeah," she said. "Timekeepers, the emperor's soldiers, something like that?"

"Something like that." Malcolm nodded. "It's what they called us in Rome, but the origin is much older. A long time ago, when the world was first made, the ancient wolves guarded the passages—the dark roads between time and space. We policed the borders between the worlds and guarded the boundaries of the abyss. But during the waning days of the empire, the Guard was corrupted by a Silver Blood emperor, Lucifer, who was called Caligula then. The Dark Prince used the wolves to find the paths of the dead so he could free the demons from the underworld and hold dominion over both earth and Hell. When we realized what he meant to do, we lent our power to Michael and his angels to build the Gates of Hell. But during the Crisis, we were betrayed by Romulus, our beloved general, who delivered us to Lucifer, who enslaved us and turned us into hounds as punishment for our insubordination. Before we were cursed, however, we were able to destroy the chronologs and the memories of the passages to keep them safe.

"Right before we escaped from Hell, Lawson heard that Romulus had found something important. We noticed that the general had taken to wearing an amulet around his neck, something silver and shiny. Rumor had it that it was a chronolog, that one of the packs had found one."

"What is it?" Bliss asked. "Is it like a watch?"

Malcolm nodded. "Sort of, it's a tool that the ancient wolves used to travel through time, a relic from the old empire. It guides you through the passages. All the guards used to have one, it was part of the arsenal." He sighed. "Anyway, there's been a lot of movement in the under-world—rumors that Lucifer is after more than just mid-world, that he's planning to storm the Gates of Paradise themselves. With the chronolog in hand, if Romulus ever found an entrance to the passages, the Dark Prince could control time itself, and become the master of all creation."

"That can't happen," Bliss said. Understatement of the century, she thought. Perhaps of all time. "So you guys didn't just escape because you were going to be turned into hounds; you wanted to stop Romulus from using the passages to help Lucifer."

"Yep," Malcolm said. "If Romulus and his armies could roam the passages, with the ability to alter time, we knew the world was no longer safe. We heard Lucifer had already given him orders—Romulus was to return to the beginning of Rome, to the founding of the empire, during the feast of Neptune."

"Why then?"

"We don't know. But we knew we had to do something. Lawson decided he had to act, find a way to break out of Hell, find the passages before Romulus did, and guard them from him. When we broke out of Hell, Lawson kept a portal open for the others to escape."

"But no one has," Rafe added. "No one but us."

"That's where you're wrong," Ahramin interrupted. She had been listening to their conversation all along,

Bliss realized, even as she had been arguing with Lawson. "Like I keep telling your brother here, you guys aren't the only wolves who've escaped from Hell."

Lawson shook his head. "It cannot be, I returned to the rendezvous again and again. I never found any others. Not a single soul."

"Maybe your portal doesn't always let out at the same place ... ever think of that?" Ahramin asked. "Maybe when they crossed, they didn't end up at the same location that you did."

"It's possible," Lawson admitted. "I barely know how the portals work myself. Or why I'm the only wolf able to make them."

"Believe me, when I was a hound under Romulus's command, yours was not the only pack we were tracking. There were many others. Marrok—"

"Marrok! Why didn't you say so earlier? He escaped?" Lawson said. His eyes were bright—Bliss saw a ray of hope begin to return to his face. She was glad for him, glad that he had found something to live for, and glad that she hadn't made a scene that morning. It was irrelevant—what had happened between them the night before—to what was at stake here. But still, would it kill him to acknowledge it with a glance in her direction?

Ahramin gazed at him evenly. "Yes. Why are you so

surprised? It was his plan all along, wasn't it? For you to lead us out of the underworld and for him to follow with the others?"

"Was he successful?" Lawson asked, standing from his seat and in his excitement almost knocking his chair to the ground.

"Are you asking me if he has the chronolog? If he was successful in stealing it from Romulus?"

Malcolm gasped. "That's a suicide mission," he whispered to Bliss.

"That was the plan—you knew it as well as I do." Lawson frowned.

"And I was the only part that failed, wasn't I?" Ahramin said. "The only one who got left behind, got caught, who got turned into this."

"Ahramin . . ."

"I have no time for self-pity. What is done is done. But if you really want to know, yes, the white wolf has the timekeeper, and he is aboveground."

TWENTY-FOUR

Ahramin stubbed her cigarette into her half-eaten doughnut, the sugar sizzling upon contact with the ashes. Lawson watched as Edon wordlessly picked it up and tossed it into the trash. His brother was trying to make it up to her, but Lawson knew it would take much more than being Ahramin's penitent servant to win back her love. Ahramin seemed to enjoy Edon's misery, and ordered him to the corner store to buy her more cigarettes before they left the hotel.

She spun a lovely tale, one he was desperate to believe. Could it be true? That the plan had worked after all? That more wolves had escaped? That Marrok had been able to steal Romulus's chronolog? Ahramin had run with the pack that hunted the white wolf—and she alone knew where the wolves were hiding, the hounds had an idea, but she had left before revealing his location to her masters; she could take Lawson to Marrok now if he wanted. If he trusted her. But what if it was all an elaborate plot to serve them up on a silver platter for Romulus's taking?

There was no such thing as former hellhounds, he knew. Only dead ones.

And yet . . . he had helped her out of the hospital; he had let her back into his pack. The brothers had accepted it—he was alpha now; he made the decisions for them, decisions they did not question. She swore that she was no longer a hound, that Romulus had broken her collar. But why was she alive, then? He had never heard of a hound surviving such an ordeal—even Ahramin had admitted as much. She was almost daring him to disbelieve her. Daring him to trust her again.

"Lawson?" Bliss said, breaking his reverie. "I'm going to go check out, okay? Boys? Want to come with me?" she asked. Malcolm and Rafe nodded, following at her heels like lovesick puppies, Lawson noted.

As if he had acted any differently, Lawson thought, feeling his face flush a little. What was that all about— the previous night? He couldn't think about his growing attraction to Bliss; his stomach twisted at the thought of it. He had wanted her the night before, that much was clear, and he still wanted her that day, he realized, watching her tall, slim form as she moved gracefully through the parking lot back to the hotel with his brothers. He hadn't wanted to stop what they were doing—and he wasn't entirely sure he was glad that they had, that she'd had the sense to stop it before they reached the point of no return. He remembered the way her body moved against his, his hands in her hair . . . but it was too confusing to think about Bliss right then. There was Tala to think of . . . Tala . . . who was with Romulus now.

As if she had read his mind, Ahramin spoke. "I wonder what Tala would say if she could see you now. With *Bliss*." She hissed the name, then almost choked from a fit of coughing.

"I'm not 'with Bliss,' so she wouldn't say anything," he said, trying not to sound defensive. "There's nothing to see. Nothing to say."

"Right. I noticed she didn't sleep in her bed last night."

He crushed his coffee cup. "I have no idea what you're talking about."

"You're such a bad liar, Lawson. You always were," she said. "But your secret's safe with me."

"I don't have any secrets," he said shortly.

Ahramin raised an eyebrow but said nothing.

"What are you guys talking about?" Bliss asked, returning to the van. "We're all set. We can go."

"Where are we going?" Ahramin asked Lawson. "Marrok is a day's drive from here, and we'll have to hike the rest of the way through the canyons. We should be there by nightfall. If he hasn't moved his pack, that is."

Lawson had to make a decision. "You will take us to the white wolf. If what you say is true, we have wasted too much time already. If Marrok *is* here, he will need our help."

The group dispersed to the restrooms before the drive, but Lawson noticed Bliss hanging back. He turned to her. "You want to ride shotgun?"

She nodded and looked as if she wanted to say something more. She hesitated, then finally asked, "Are you sure about this?"

"I know what you're thinking. You don't think we should trust Ahri," he said.

"No, I don't. You told me when you were hurt that wolves never get sick, that disease and infection have no effect on you guys—but she coughs all the time. It's not just from the smoking. What's that all about?"

"I noticed it too. I don't know." He crossed his arms. "But I believe she's not a hound anymore, Romulus broke her collar. You saw the scars on her neck."

"If you say so," Bliss said.

"She's still one of us," Lawson said. "I have to believe that."

"Why?"

"During our escape from Hell, Ahramin sacrificed herself so that we would be free." He cleared his throat. "She gave herself up willingly, and I have to honor that sacrifice. I have to believe . . . that what she says is true, that there *is* still wolf in her." He took a deep breath. What he had to say would pain Bliss, he knew. She had stopped them from taking things too far the night before because he had a feeling she had wanted it to mean something more, something that he was not yet prepared to give, given the circumstances. He stared at the ground, at the gray gravel in front of him, not able to look into her eyes. "I have to believe Ahramin is still a wolf. Because if Tala has been turned, if she is a hound, I have to believe that she can return to me."

Bliss took a deep breath. She patted his arm. "Of course. I would feel the same way if . . . " She was thinking of the boy she had once loved, Lawson knew. "But let's just . . . be careful."

He smiled at her. They were a team now, and he marveled at how quickly they had formed a deep understanding of each other in such a short time, from combatants to lovers to friends. "Always."

TWENTY-FIVE

*B*liss couldn't recall ever seeing a sky so black or stars so bright, with the moon hanging so low over the trees. The drive had been long and wearisome, and as they'd been warned, the hike was steep and treacherous. They had locked Arthur's van and left it at the base of the mountain, off the road, hidden in a copse of trees. Ahramin led the way as they walked through the woods, following a road up a long valley, over a pair of hills. Edon tried to keep up with her pace; Rafe and Malcolm followed them, with Lawson and Bliss at the rear. In the moonlight she could see that Lawson looked troubled. He had not spoken very much on the drive, and now she saw he had retreated deeper into himself, his brow furrowed, as he put one foot in front of the other, trudging along. They reached the crest of the first hill and looked down at the valley below, and Bliss heard Lawson suck in the air through his teeth. She turned to him and saw his face pale under the moonlight.

"What's wrong?" They were looking down at a strange formation on the ground below, with the body of a snake, an oval shape at its head.

Lawson squinted and shook his head. "I have a strange feeling. Mac," he whispered to his brother up ahead. "What is that thing? It looks familiar, like I've seen it before."

"You have," Malcolm confirmed, making his way back to them. "An old diorama of it, anyway. There's one in Arthur's show cave. It's a serpent mound." He explained what he knew, that the serpent mound was of Native American origin, built more than eight hundred years ago by an unnamed Paleo-Indian tribe. Its shape was made to celebrate the solstices, the body of the serpent aligned with the positions of the summer and winter suns.

The Indian burial mound was a man-made hill covered in dense grass, and Bliss could see that the serpent had three parts. It started with the tail, a winding spiral in three arcs that straightened near the head, which was triangular and made to look as if the snake had its mouth open. Inside the serpent's jaw was an oval pit dug into the earth. In the center of the excavation was a black rock.

"That's not it ... there's something more," Lawson said. "That serpent mound ... I'm pretty sure it's an entrance to the passages. The wolves must have found it and dug it out."

Malcolm whistled. "The dark roads? The *Via Obscuris*? Here?"

Lawson nodded. "The portal was supposed to bring us close to it when we crossed from the underworld ... Marrok had a feeling it would be here. It looks like he was right. Do you notice the circle and stone inside the snake's mouth?"

Bliss and Malcolm nodded.

"I'm pretty sure that conceals an entrance to the passages. The earthwork was a warning, built to ward off anyone who might disturb the site, to keep the portal closed."

Ahramin led them down the mountain toward it. Their footsteps crunched on the dirt and gravel. It was slow going; the path twisted and turned, and the slippery grass made it hard for them to keep their balance. Bliss felt her legs ache from the strain of keeping herself upright on the down slope. There was no sign of movement in the trees, no sign of wolves. If Lawson was right and the serpent mound concealed an entrance to the passages, what did it mean? Wasn't Romulus searching for this? Could it mean that the hounds were nearby? Bliss was more and more worried that Ahramin was leading them into a trap.

The silence was broken by a loud, rasping cough and Bliss startled.

"I'm okay," Malcolm said, turning around. "Sorry to scare everyone."

They picked their way through tall grasses that flanked the narrow path that wound down the steep incline, and they found themselves surrounded on both sides by high stone walls that shadowed the night sky. The cliffs were easily a hundred feet high, but only a dozen feet apart. The path between felt like an alley between skyscrapers, dark and tight. It was hard to move and impossible to see around the next corner. The serpent mound was at the end of it, Bliss realized, the gorge forming a natural protection.

If the wolves were here, they had chosen a good hiding place. Anyone who approached would need to wade slowly through the narrow passageway. The crackling shale floor slowly disappeared beneath a thick coat of watery muck. Bliss felt her feet sinking into the mud and was glad she'd worn boots that laced tightly. She heard

Lawson curse as he tried to walk but found that his boot was stuck. When he pulled up his foot, he was shoeless.

"Everything all right back there?" Edon whispered from the vanguard.

"Miserable place for a midnight walk," Lawson muttered.

Bliss couldn't agree more. She was knee-deep in the coarse muck, unable to move as freezing water poured over her legs. It flowed through the mud and dripped down the loose shale walls. There was only the sound of water dripping.

Then Malcolm dry-heaved.

She exchanged stricken glances with Lawson, who stood frozen, still holding his shoe. "No one move," Lawson whispered as he pushed his way toward her through the mud, retrieved boot in hand.

Bliss held her breath as Lawson looked right, then left. What was it he'd told her earlier? Hellhounds faded in the sunlight. They were easier to see in the dark. She squinted. She couldn't see anything. "Where are they?" she asked.

"I don't know . . . I can't hear them. Malcolm?"

The youngest boy shook his head, wiped his mouth with his sleeve. "I'm not sure. I thought I felt something . . ."

"Where's Ahramin?" Lawson demanded, noticing they were missing one member of the group.

"She was here a moment ago ... " Edon replied. "You don't think ... " He shook his head, his forehead crinkling with worry. "No ... she couldn't ... she wouldn't ... "

Before anyone could answer, there was a scramble in the darkness. A roar, a growl, a flash of teeth in the dark. "There!" Bliss cried, seeing the dark girl appear out of the shadows. Lawson leapt, turning into a wolf to chase her down, but someone else got there first.

There was a flash of white, and Ahramin lay on the ground, paralyzed. Edon ran to her but he was shot down just as easily.

Bliss looked around as she and Rafe shielded Malcolm behind them. All around them, in the darkness, dark shapes began to emerge from the shadows. But the beasts did not have the telltale silver and crimson markings of the hellhounds.

"Wolves," she breathed. They were hiding in the earth, blending in with the black mud of the riverbed. She could see them now as they moved out of the darkness. Their lupine forms changed into human features, until they stood in front of them as boys and girls in ragged clothing. She could see their resemblance to Lawson and his brothers.

The group parted and a boy walked between them. His hair was platinum—Bliss realized he had been the white flash they had seen—and his eyes were strangely colorless, not quite silver or white, but clear. Marrok, the white wolf. He made his way to where Ahramin was lying next to Edon.

Lawson was kneeling by them, breathing heavily, but Marrok did not see him. He went straight to Ahramin and looked down at her with contempt. "Why, Ulric, you were right. It *is* Ahramin of the Hounds. Romulus's favorite huntress."

Bliss gripped Malcolm's hand tightly, but no one said a word; they were all trained on Marrok.

Ahramin struggled against the invisible restraints that held her. "Marrok—please. I wore a collar then. I understand your anger, but you must listen to me," she begged, coughing and gurgling.

"Why? So you can seduce me again? So you can lie and trick me into spying for the masters like you did in the underworld?" He placed his foot on her chest, but he didn't appear to be bearing down on her; he was merely making sure she was still unable to move.

"I was only doing as I was told. It was not my fault, just as you had no choice when you slew your own kin when you escaped."

In answer, he spit on the ground by her feet. Marrok turned to his wolves. "Ulric, Blaez, take this garbage away. Before she alerts the hounds to our presence." Then he looked around, as if noticing the rest of them for the first time.

"Marrok, my friend," Lawson said, a tense smile on his face.

"Ulf!" Marrok said. "What took you so long? And what are you doing with this traitor?"

PART FOUR

If you're lost you can look and you will find me.

Cyndi Lauper, "Time After Time"

TWENTY-SIX

"It's Lawson now," he said as Marrok helped him to his feet.

"New world, new name," the white wolf said. "Makes sense." Marrok nodded as two large, burly boys picked up Ahramin and Edon and took them into the forest.

"Where are you taking them?" Lawson asked. "One of them is my brother."

"Do not worry, no harm will come to him, but I cannot promise the same for the hound." Marrok turned to Rafe and Malcolm. "There is food and drink in the camp. Go and find your friends. There are many from your den with us."

Marrok was striking, Bliss thought, but his beauty was marred by an ugly raised scar that bisected his face.

"A gift from Romulus," he said when he caught her eye.

"I'm sorry—I didn't mean to stare," Bliss said as Marrok turned his head to reveal the full scope of the burn that ravaged his face and neck.

"It's a wound that will never heal, but it reminds me not to take things for granted. I wear the mark with pride." He clasped his hands together. "Come," he said. "There is much to discuss, but we must have a good meal first." He looked at Bliss with narrowed eyes. "Your mate?" he asked Lawson.

"No—just a friend," Lawson replied while Bliss looked away, trying not to blush.

"You were like one of the masters once," Marrok said, studying her face. "Yet you are one of us now. You have a wolflike quality about you. Why is that?" He did not seem bothered by her, only curious.

"It's a long story," she said. She couldn't help staring at his strange, colorless eyes. He was pale, almost like an albino.

"Perhaps you will share it with me someday," Marrok said, and his tone of voice suggested he would like that very much.

Lawson smirked. "Stop flirting, you old dog. Get us something to eat."

Marrok led them past the serpent mound toward a

group of trees that seemed tall enough to block the sun. Bliss found it difficult to know where to look first—the wolves had managed to create some sort of architectural miracle that seemed almost like an optical illusion. She was reminded of some M. C. Escher drawings, with their stair-cases that looped up and down, twisting and turning in ways that weren't entirely real. The wolves seemed to have woven the leaves and branches into a community of nest-like shapes connected with rope ladders that looped up and down and around the trunks of even the tallest trees.

Her appreciation of the architectural beauty of it quickly turned to panic, though, as she realized that it would be impossible for her to reach even the lowest of the nest-like enclosures. She was about to ask Lawson what she should do, but discovered with a start that when she turned her head, the hive formation was gone.

She turned back to look at it and found it unchanged, and turned to Lawson again, only to see it all disappear.

Lawson noticed her confusion and smiled. "It's an old wolves' trick," he said. "Using humans' peripheral vision against them. This camp is only visible to humans if they look at it directly, and even then, they probably won't believe what they see, especially if it disappears when they turn their heads. It's a way of hiding in plain sight."

"Clever." She nodded.

He helped her climb the trees, teaching her where to place her feet, how to lift herself up with her hands. Marrok climbed ahead, leading them to a platform balanced precariously on the top of the boughs.

"What is this place?" Bliss asked.

"It's where I was supposed to meet Marrok, when we first escaped from the underworld," Lawson said. "I thought he would come out at the same place we did, and it turned out I was waiting at the wrong place. It looks like they've been here for a while."

On the platform, a meal had been prepared. "I hope you don't mind an early dinner," Marrok said. "Since we gained our freedom, we've tried to keep some of the old Roman traditions alive, so our main meal is the *cena*, the late-afternoon meal."

"I'd eat anything at this point," Lawson said.

They sat cross-legged in front of a basket of bread and a plate of roasted meat. For a while, no one spoke as they focused their attention on eating.

Lawson finally pushed his plate away. "I gave up on you," he said. "I thought there was no hope."

"I'm sorry we were a bit delayed. We had some trouble," Marrok murmured.

"Ahramin."

"We were not privy to the details of your escape, we

did not know that Ahramin had been captured. The hounds sent her to our den. We trusted her. But she was already one of them. Luckily one of us noticed the crimson around her pupils and we told her nothing. When they realized she was useless as a spy, they sent her aboveground. We only managed to escape after she'd gone. We tried to find you when we got here, but kept missing your scent. I'm glad you found us."

"I thought we were alone," Lawson said. "I thought we were the only ones who made it out. But then we found Ahramin, and she said there were other free wolves. I didn't know what to believe; I thought it might be a trick, I wasn't sure what I would find when we got here."

"Ahramin ..." Marrok shrugged. "She is a traitor. We have been looking for her since Romulus unleashed her on us."

"She says Romulus broke her collar, that she is no longer a servant of the beast," Lawson said. "She led us to you. I would never have come back otherwise."

"She might be playing a more complicated game with you. With us."

Lawson reached for a piece of bread and tore it with his fingers, crushing part of it into a yeasty ball. "If you release her to Edon, I can promise that he'll keep an eye on her."

"Edon, who loves her so desperately he won't leave her side? I think not."

"She's part of my pack," Lawson said.

"Ulf, you are my friend, but I'm sorry," Marrok said, "there's nothing she can do that will make up for how she betrayed us."

Lawson sighed. "You have the chronolog?"

"It wasn't easy," Marrok said as he broke off a piece of bread and nibbled on it.

"Fenrir raise his ugly head?" Lawson asked. "Is that how you got it?"

The light-haired boy shook his head and smiled. "I'm telling you, that's a myth."

"Who's Fenrir?" asked Bliss.

Lawson explained that there was a legend among the wolves that one day the great wolf Fenrir would return and free them from slavery. It was something wolf cubs told each other, especially during those last desperate days before they would be turned into hounds . . . that one day they would return to their former glory . . . that one day, someone would come . . . someone would be sent . . . to help them . . . to free them. "Just another old wolves' tale," he said, smiling. "Obviously we didn't need anyone to free us from the underworld. We freed ourselves. How many more wolves managed to escape?" he asked Marrok.

"Not as many as we'd like, much less than we'd hoped," Marrok said. "A centuria at most."

"Where are they?"

"Scattered. The hounds hunt us day and night; many of us have been captured and sent back."

"How many are here?"

Marrok shrugged. "Fifty, sixty at most. You saw the entrance to the passages, I assume? The serpent mound?"

"Yes." Lawson nodded.

"The dark roads have returned to us," Marrok said. "The power of the wolves is growing"

"So it would seem," Lawson said.

Marrok took a long drink from his goblet. "There's something more you should know. We have been tracking the hounds as well, to avoid their movements. One of our spies found this in the remnants of their camp. I think it belongs to you?" He handed it to Lawson.

Lawson stared at it in his palm. It was a small gold chain with a heart locket, engraved with a crescent moon. A trinket from the mall, a cheap little thing, but Tala had wanted it and he had given it to her. She always wore it; she never took it off. Someone must have pulled it off her neck, must have broken the chain.

"It's Tala's, isn't it?" Bliss asked.

"Yes." Romulus was taunting him, Lawson thought;

Romulus knew the wolves were tracking the hounds, and he'd meant for someone to find it, to bring it back to Lawson. Romulus wanted Lawson to know he held her life in his hands. Wanted Lawson to come to him to rescue her. Wanted Lawson to show himself, wanted to bring him closer.

"Tala, who escaped with you?" Marrok asked.

Lawson nodded. "But she did not get away the second time. When the hounds returned."

"We did not see a wolf in their midst, but we could be wrong. Their numbers are great. Our spies tell me that Romulus's pack is making its way here. They will be upon us in a day or two."

"They are close, then—that must have been why Malcolm felt ill," Lawson said.

Marrok continued. "He is gathering his hounds for Rome, to the beginning of the empire's founding, as Lucifer wanted. The loss of the chronolog hasn't changed or slowed his plan, but I don't understand how he presumes to navigate the dark roads without one. Without a chronolog to guide them, the passages are useless. He must know something we don't."

Lawson ruminated on the news, still holding the small gold chain tightly. "Let him find the passages. Let him come."

Marrok frowned. "What are you saying? I've sent a call to the wolves to defend the passages from him."

But Lawson was adamant. The light was back in his eyes, and his voice was confident. "When Romulus and his hounds arrive, we will let them inside the passages. *Let them go to Rome.* I will take my pack after and follow him inside."

"What?" Bliss cried out.

"I'm with her," Marrok said. "Why?"

"Outside of Hell, Romulus is vulnerable. Especially in Rome, he will have to retain human form. He will be weaker. Don't you see? We can kill him, Marrok. I know we can. We must strike now. This might be our only chance."

"Kill an ancient wolf? You forget he is immortal. Only we new pups die like ants crushed beneath a heel."

"I did not forget," Lawson said. He removed a small velvet pouch and showed them the needle inside it, which had unlocked their collars in the underworld. "I still have this." Before their eyes, it grew to the size of a sword, shining golden in the moonlight.

"That is Michael's sword," Bliss breathed. "An archangel's blade. But it was broken," she said, remembering how the glass she had held had shattered into a million pieces.

201

"A heavenly blade is never broken, the masters found it after a great battle aboveground," Lawson explained. "It was the deadliest weapon in Hell's arsenal. It carries the White Fire of Heaven." The Hand of God, it was known as among the creatures of the underworld.

"It can kill that which cannot be killed," Bliss murmured, thinking of the blood the sword had shed. Of how it had been used for ill gain. Of the vampires who had fallen to its power. It was the sword that had killed Lawrence Van Alen. It was the sword that she had plunged into her own heart, breaking her father's hold on her spirit.

"It can kill Romulus and it will," Lawson said, gritting his teeth. "I swear it."

TWENTY-SEVEN

*A*t the end of the meal, Marrok bid them good night. "You will be safe here," he promised. "Until daybreak, then."

Lawson left Bliss as well to check on his brothers. She found a few worn blankets at the edge of the platform and settled down to rest, although sleep did not come easily. Lawson's plan worried her. He was so certain he could bring down Romulus and maybe even rescue Tala. Was Tala in a position to be rescued? Bliss thought of the ugly black scar on Ahramin's neck and shuddered. Lawson was filled with hope now, and it was driving his decisions, but that didn't mean his plan had any chance of succeeding. And if it didn't succeed, Lawson and his brothers were headed for either death or captivity. She wasn't sure which was worse.

On top of everything else, Bliss had a larger purpose for finding the pack in the first place. She was supposed to tame the wolves, to bring them back to the fold. How was she going to do that if her friends—and even though she had just met them, she knew they were her friends—were captured or dead? Jane was still missing too, and they weren't any closer to finding her.

Bliss sat up with a start. It had just occurred to her how Jane was connected to the hounds. What was it that Marrok had said about the passages?

I don't understand how he presumes to navigate the dark roads without the chronolog.

Then it occurred to her. The answer wasn't *what* Romulus would use; it was who. She had to find Lawson and tell him immediately. She scaled down the trees, finding her footing in the dark. She followed the murmur of familiar voices and found Lawson, Rafe, and Malcolm huddled in a lower enclosure.

"Hey, Bliss," Malcolm said, smiling. "Cool to be around all the wolves, right? Almost feels like home."

"Edon still with Ahramin?" she asked.

"Yeah, he won't leave her even though they're not holding *him* in a cage. We just checked on them. They're both fine," Rafe said. "A bit irritable, but that's to be expected."

"I was about to go up," Lawson said to her. "You climbed down all by yourself?"

She nodded. "I couldn't wait. I figured out something important."

"What's up?"

"You told them what Marrok said? About Romulus's plans not changing?" she asked. The boys nodded. "Okay. It's about Aunt Jane. She was the Watcher. The *Pistis Sophia*," she said. "The Immortal Intelligence of the Blue Blood Coven. She's a seer. Marrok said he didn't know how Romulus planned to make his way through the passages without the chronolog. Well, after Marrok stole the chronolog, Romulus stole something too; he stole Aunt Jane. He's planning to use the Watcher to navigate through time. It's why the hounds took her. It has to be."

"You never mentioned that before," Lawson said. "The Watcher, huh? What does that mean?"

"I'm sorry ... it's complicated." Bliss explained, as quickly as she could, Jane's various incarnations, among them the sister of Lucifer, and how she'd now returned in the form of Jane Murray, the woman Bliss called Aunt Jane. "I thought the hounds took her to keep me off their scent," she said. "But now I think they took her because of who she was, not because of who I am."

"Have you heard about this *Pistis Sophia*?" Lawson asked Malcolm.

"No, but that doesn't mean anything," Malcolm said. "But I'm guessing it's most likely because this Watcher is something the vampires keep a closely guarded secret. An oracle who can predict the return of the Dark Prince is not something they would reveal to the rest of the world."

"So ... this Immortal Intelligence can make the chronolog unnecessary?" Lawson asked.

"I'm not sure, but I'm guessing yes, it could."

"I can see where stealing her would be easier than getting the chronolog back from Marrok," he mused. "Can they make her do it, though? Would his powers work on someone like that?"

"I don't know," Bliss admitted. She wasn't sure what Jane was capable of, didn't know how long she could resist them.

Lawson must have seen the distress on her face. He reached over and put a hand on her shoulder. "We'll find her," he said softly. "If she's been through that much in her many lifetimes, she'll make it through this. We'll find her, and we'll bring her back to you."

"Thank you," she said.

He smiled at her, looking handsome and regal even as he was sitting in the dirt, leaning against the tree. He began to empty his pockets, just like a boy, Bliss thought; they always removed their wallets and phones when they sat down. He tossed a stack of pictures held together by a rubber band on the ground.

"Could I see that?" she asked.

She picked up the stack and looked through the pictures. In the middle was the postcard she had seen before. It was the image of a painting showing a riotous struggle between an army of Roman centurions and a defenseless crowd of women. One figure, however, stood motionless and calm at the top of the scene. He wore red robes, carried a staff, and held a single hand aloft.

"Romulus," Lawson said, tapping the picture. "I've always been drawn to this painting; one of the stories passed down among the wolves is about our history with the Sabines, but I don't know much about it. None of us do, we just know we're connected to them somehow. I found this in a gift shop and I had to have it."

"I know a little bit," Bliss said. She had studied history with Jane Murray, and she remembered what her aunt had told her about the event.

"Tell me."

"During the founding of Rome, the Romans took the

Sabines as wives. They were a soldiers' society and women were scarce. They needed to balance the population and so they had to abduct their wives from the surrounding communities. They planned celebratory games for their new city and called the festival the Consualia, a festival for Neptune. It was intended to attract people from the surrounding region, act as a showcase for the newly built city of Rome. They issued invitations to all the tribes, including the Sabines. But it was just a cover. As the games were about to begin, Romulus gave the signal that you see here, and the Roman soldiers rushed into the crowd and snatched the unarmed Sabine women." She looked closely at the picture. "Something's different. Something's changed," she said. "Look!"

"I don't see any difference," Lawson said, squinting at it.

"There is—they're *killing* the women in this version— stabbing them, gutting them." Bliss turned the postcard over. In small print, the text read *The Massacre of the Sabine Women*.

But when she turned the postcard back, the image was the original painting, in which the women were merely being captured. The title went back to the original as well.

"It's changed back—what's going on?" Bliss asked.

"You can see that?" Lawson asked. He looked at her keenly. "I'm not sure, but I think what we're seeing is a timeline in flux. History hasn't been set. Something's happened or is about to happen. This must be where Romulus is headed when he enters the passages. He's going to this moment in time to turn the abduction into a massacre. But why? Why does Lucifer want the Sabines destroyed? Why are they so important?"

TWENTY-EIGHT

*I*n the morning, Lawson told his brothers the plan to follow Romulus into the timeline. "I don't expect you to follow me, I can handle him myself," he said.

"What do you take us for, cowards?" Rafe asked. "Of course we are going with you. Right, Mac?"

Malcolm nodded. "We followed you out of the underworld, we will follow you back to Rome."

Lawson nodded his thanks and it was clear he had not expected anything less. "Come on, let's go see the chief," he said.

Marrok listened patiently as Bliss told her story. "So, Romulus has found himself a guide to the passages," he said. "Let us hope she is not as good as this one." He pulled something from his pocket. It was a small round silver pocket watch in a cloth handkerchief. "We were immune to the silver once, but not anymore. I will give this to you to hold, since I don't think it will burn your skin." He dropped the watch into her palm. It was unusually heavy and cold.

Bliss looked down at the chronolog. The dial had Roman numerals numbered from one to twenty-four. The numerals started at the bottom of the dial and moved counterclockwise around the circle. There was a second dial, layered over the first, in silver, and the edge of the watch face was carved with runes. "How do you use it?"

"We're not sure," Marrok said, embarrassed. "I'm hoping it will be self-explanatory once all of you enter the passages."

Bliss touched the chronolog and suddenly experienced a flash of memory. In her mind, she saw a hand reach out and press a button on the side of the chronolog. But it wasn't her hand, and she wasn't accessing her own memories; they belonged to someone else. Not Lucifer—she didn't have the icy feeling that crept up her spine when she knew she was recalling something he'd seen. No, these were pleasant memories, memories of a happier time and place, memories belonging to someone she loved. This memory was Allegra's. She blinked and looked around. How strange that she had her mother's memories in her as well. It comforted her to know she still had a connection to Allegra.

"Can I see it?" Malcolm asked shyly.

"Careful," she said, placing it on his palm with a handkerchief.

Lawson was arguing with Marrok. "I told you last night, I'm not leaving without Ahramin. She's part of my pack. Release her to me."

Marrok did not look happy to hear that. "You don't know what she did down there. She was the worst one they had, Lawson. She was vicious . . . cruel. She's not the she-wolf she was. They turned her into a hound."

"Even so, they turned her into something else when Romulus broke her collar. She's not a hound anymore. Her eyes are blue. She cannot shift. Marrok, be reasonable."

"She tortured us, Ulf. Not reluctantly—with glee. When they released her aboveground, she tracked us one by one. Wasn't she the hound who found your pack?"

Lawson did not answer. Of course he remembered. The dark girl at the door, her eyes blazing with crimson hatred. "She wore a collar back then. She doesn't now. She's part of my pack. I speak for her."

Marrok sighed. "There's no other way?"

"She belongs with us. My brother will not leave her side. Without her, I lose Edon. I will need all my strength when I go to Rome."

"I understand," Marrok said. "I will release her to your care. But she is your responsibility now. If she betrays us, my pack will not hesitate to kill her."

"If she betrays us," Lawson promised, "I'll kill her myself."

Ahramin did not seem grateful that Lawson had pled her release. The wolves had been holding her in a wooden cage, and the bars exhaled as they clattered to the ground. She stepped over the wooden sticks. "Marrok had every right to hold me, you don't know what I did for Romulus," Ahramin said dully. "Why did you secure my freedom?" she asked Lawson.

"I trust you, Ahramin. You brought us to Marrok, to the free wolves, as you had promised. You say you are no longer a hound and I believe you," he said, offering his hand to shake. "Peace?"

Her eyes flashed but she held her tongue and managed to shake his hand. Bliss hoped Lawson knew what he was doing. Ahramin made her way to Edon, who had never left her side, who had slept next to her cage all night.

"I know he only asked for my freedom because of you," she said to him, sounding tender toward him for the first time since she had returned to the pack. She held a hand to his cheek, and Edon put a hand on top of hers. They stood there for a long time. Whatever had broken between them appeared to be mending.

As Bliss watched the two of them, she felt another stab of jealousy. It was another reminder that Dylan was gone, forever this time, and the one person who made his absence hurt a little less was obsessed with finding his own lost love. She could never compete with that, and she wouldn't want to.

The pretty scene was broken by Malcolm's vomiting all over his shoes. He fell to the ground and began to shake all over, his body jerking in spasms. Rafe picked him up in his arms. "It's bad, they must be right on us," he said.

"Into the pine trees. Now!" Lawson said as he led them into the forest, where the thicket of trees was dense and could protect them from being seen. Bliss huddled down and held her hands around her knees. "How many?" she asked.

"A whole legion, it seems like," Lawson whispered. "Poor Mac."

There was a rustling that slowly turned into the sound of an army approaching; Bliss got scared. She grabbed Lawson's arm to steady herself, and he pulled her toward him, his arm around her shoulders, her head resting in the crook of his neck.

"It's okay," he said. "We're going to get through this."

Then came the sound of heavy boots, and the hounds appeared. They were fearsome and massive in the dim twilight. Their crimson-and-silver eyes shone, and their armor clanked loudly. There were hundreds of them and they roared past, heading toward the serpent mound. They kept coming—they leapt from branches and tore through the tall grasses, bounding over the low earthen mounds until they were out of sight.

"Let's go," Lawson said. He signaled to his brothers and the team raced through the woods and down the side of the mountain, to the serpent mound.

Marrok was waiting for them at the serpent's mouth. Around him were nearly a hundred wolves in their animal form, clawing the ground and howling. "You sure about this?" he asked Lawson. "That was an entire legion we just let inside."

Lawson nodded. "There will be more." He turned to Bliss, Ahramin, and his brothers. "Ready?"

They nodded.

"Where are we going?" Ahramin asked.

"Shh—" Edon warned. "We will go where Lawson leads us."

"Well, then, there's no time like the present." Lawson turned to Marrok one last time. "You will hold them here? Keep the rest from entering the passages behind us?"

"It's our duty," Marrok said, raising his hand in farewell. "Godspeed."

Lawson raised his hand to salute Marrok and led his team into the passages.

TWENTY-NINE

Bliss followed Lawson into the mouth of the serpent, Ahramin and the boys following close behind. The path was narrow and dark, the air dusty. Ahramin started coughing again; Bliss felt almost like she needed to cough herself. She could hear Marrok's wolves battling the hounds behind them, but the further they walked down the passages, the fainter the noises became. The wolves must have been doing their job well, though, because no hounds followed them.

"Stay close," Lawson warned. "It's only going to get darker as we move away, and there's more than one path underground—we have to make sure we stay behind the hounds and find the actual entrance to the timeline. I don't want to lose anyone."

"I've got the scent," Edon said.

"Me too," said Rafe.

Bliss moved to the side and let them pass her. She ended up just ahead of Malcolm, and turned around to check on him. "How are you feeling? Still nauseous?"

"A bit," he admitted. "But I'm used to it. I don't follow scent as well as they do, so it's kind of good that I have my own way of telling when they're around, you know?"

They were now deep enough into the path that Bliss couldn't hear the wolves at all, and she could barely see. Fortunately, Lawson had brought some matches, and every so often he'd light one to make sure everyone was nearby.

The brief flicker of each match revealed that there were occasional openings to paths stemming off the one they were on. Occasionally Lawson would veer in one direction or another, and Bliss could feel that they were heading deeper and deeper into the earth. The group walked silently for what felt like hours. How deep in the earth did the timeline start? Bliss wondered. They might as well just walk to Rome.

"Everyone, brace yourselves," Lawson warned. "I think we're getting close to the passages." He explained that once they entered the timeline, they would be moving through time itself, from moment to moment, where everything happened at once, and it could be disorienting at first.

"The Praetorian Guard kept the timeline safe," he said to Bliss as they walked down the narrow space. "Time is sacred. It must not change, and the wolves saw to that. Those who tamper with the timeline are doomed. Time must be allowed to flow, the sequence of events must remain fixed."

Bliss nodded. "Otherwise ... "

"Paradox, chaos, disorder. Those who do not study history are doomed to repeat it," Lawson said, smiling.

Bliss did not smile back. "Marrok said he didn't know how to use the chronolog ... and you've never traveled through time before, have you? You said the passages were closed ... lost to the wolves."

"Are you asking me if I know what I'm doing?"

"Well, yes."

Lawson grinned. "Then the answer is no. But when do I ever?"

They walked a few more steps, and the space was suddenly flooded with light. They were no longer in the serpent mound but in the timeline itself.

Bliss shielded her eyes while Lawson yelled, "HERE WE GO!"

For the first few steps, Bliss couldn't see a thing—the light was so bright it had blinded her. Then everything changed—it was as if she had stepped on a roller coaster. She could feel her stomach drop. With each step she was in a different place, a different time. It was like moving through a movie screen but with the events of the movie actually happening. It made her feel as nauseous as Malcolm seemed.

"Look to the horizon," Lawson said. "It's a constant—like being in the sea. It will make it easier."

She nodded, trying to focus on the blue sky ahead. All around her, images and memories swirled, from many moments in time, not just from her life but from the history of the entire world. She could hear everyone around her, so at least they'd arrived safely, wherever they were. The light changed, slowly fading until she could see more comfortably. She saw Edon holding on to Ahramin as if she were about to fall; Rafe helped Malcolm. Lawson was at the head of the group.

"Bliss—the chronolog," Lawson called.

She pulled the handkerchief-wrapped object out of her pocket and carefully unwrapped it. It was a beautiful object, a pocket watch, heavy and silver.

"You'll have to do it, none of us can touch silver."

Bliss looked at it closely. There were tiny scratches on

the side that looked as if someone had tried to pry it open. She recalled Allegra's hand reaching toward it, and Bliss did the same, pressing a hidden button on the side of the watch. A small round disc appeared in midair. It looked like a spinning globe, with lines moving around it.

"What is that?" Lawson asked.

She shrugged. "I have no idea."

"I think maybe you need to tell it where you want to go," Malcolm said helpfully.

"Take us to Rome," Lawson ordered, and a passage opened before them, shining bright in the darkness.

THIRTY

*T*he light and the passage disappeared, and when Bliss opened her eyes, she saw that she was in a small stone room with bars on the windows. "Where are we? A prison?" she asked.

"No ... a monastery, I think," Lawson said, frowning. "But we're not in the right place or the right time. Look."

Bliss looked out the window to a grand canal dotted with gondolas and speedboats, people rushing about on the cobblestone streets with umbrellas.

"Where are the monks?" Ahramin asked, taking a seat on a stone step.

"They're gone, I think only the tourists are left," Malcolm said, reading a plaque by a velvet stanchion at the end of the room. "It must be Tuesday, when the museums are closed, otherwise we'd be surrounded by them."

"We're close," Bliss said, comforting Lawson. "Venice isn't too far from Rome."

"When I make portals . . . I just imagine a space in my mind . . . I thought it would be same here," he said, biting his fingernail.

"These portals you create, they must be part of the passages somehow," Bliss said.

"Maybe, I don't know. All I know is I can picture myself somewhere else, and then a path appears in front of me. I thought using the chronolog would be that easy."

Bliss nodded. She had an idea. When the Visitor, Lucifer, had taken over her mind and she'd been able to see his memories, she'd had no control; she couldn't call up a memory at will. But the images she'd seen of Allegra's memories felt different, and she wondered if maybe it was possible for her to summon them at will, if she focused hard enough. She'd have to be careful how she explained herself, though; she still wasn't sure what would happen if Lawson ever discovered her true parentage, and now wasn't the time to find out. She stared at the chronolog. "I think my mother had one of these once, and sometimes I can access her memories," she said.

"How?" Lawson asked.

She shook her head. "I don't know, all I know is I can feel her—guiding me—and I think that maybe if I concentrate, I can remember a little more, see how she used it." She took a seat on the stone step next to Ahramin, who gave her some space. Bliss closed her eyes and focused. *Tell me,* she thought. *Please, if you know anything, please tell me. Show me.*

At first all she could see was darkness. But then the darkness blurred, and a light began to shimmer, and she saw Allegra pick up the chronolog again and open it. The disc had stopped spinning and looked more like a regular watch, but with three different hands, and the numbers at the edge of the circle were in multiples of thousands, hundreds, and tens. Layered over the whole disc and its hands was a map, and Allegra maneuvered the hands on the chronolog to certain positions.

Bliss opened her eyes. "I think I know how to do this." She took the chronolog and pressed the button, then waited for the disc to stop spinning. "You see these hands?" She pointed them out. "One set refers to time, measured first in thousands and then hundreds of years, then decades. You have to set it like a clock—see this knob? You wind it so the hands move," she said, adjusting it. "Now these other hands, with the images of the continents behind them? They represent longitude and latitude. The trick is to line up the time and place you want at the same time, then press another button on the side."

"So we just have to set it to the right time and co-ordinates, then press the button and we're there," Malcolm said excitedly. "We can do this!"

"Not so fast," Lawson said. "Anyone know the date? Or the coordinates?"

Malcolm's face fell.

"We can find those things," Rafe said. "If this is a monastery, there's got to be a library here, with a set of encyclopedias."

"I'll help," Bliss said, and followed Rafe down the stairs. They walked around the empty monastery until they reached a room at the end of the hallway that was blocked off from museum tours. "I think this is it," Rafe said, opening the door marked BIBLIOTHECA.

The room was covered with dust and lined with book-shelves. A little typewriter sat on an antique desk. Rafe whistled, and nodded to a shelf that contained a full set of the *Encyclopædia Britannica*. What she wouldn't give for the Internet right now, she thought; they'd have their questions answered in seconds.

"I'll look up the year, you take the location. Okay?" she asked Rafe.

"Sounds good to me."

Rafe's job was easier, she knew—all he had to do was look up Italy and he'd find everything he needed, and he did. "The coordinates for Rome are latitude 41 degrees 54 minutes north and longitude 12 degrees 30 minutes east." He smiled at Bliss. "Malcolm will be able to figure out how to set it if we can't."

Her task was trickier—she had to figure out the year of the feast in which Romulus had held the first Neptunalia, when the Sabine women were captured. Should she look up Rome? Romulus? Neptunalia? Sabine women? She finally found what she was looking for in an entry entitled "The Rape of the Sabine Women." She realized that later scholars changed their theories about what had really happened on that day—and that "rape" had been just another word for "kidnapping," which was why the painting had been called *The Abduction of the Sabine Women* when she'd seen it in the museum.

"Have you found anything?" Rafe asked.

"Almost there," she said. The information was pretty confusing, and she wasn't sure how trustworthy the date the encyclopedia listed was. "It says eighth century BC, but the dates are a little vague. As best as I can tell, it was 752 BC. I'd hate to be off, though—who knows where we'd end up?"

"If that's the best information we can find, it's better than nothing," Rafe said.

They headed back to find the group in heated discussion. "We're trying to figure out what Romulus has to gain by killing all of those women," Lawson said.

"Does anyone have a theory?" asked Bliss.

"Not exactly. But I'm pretty sure it has to do with all the things that have been changing lately. It's not just the Gates of Hell that are falling—that's part of it, but it's more than that," Lawson said.

"Like what?"

"Mac, you want to take this one?" Edon said.

"The oculi being lit, the dark roads being discovered. Like Marrok said, they seem to be signs that the power of the wolves is returning, and I think Lucifer wants to go back and stop it. If the wolves get their power back, it will be harder, if not impossible, to keep turning us into hellhounds," Malcolm said.

"The ancient wolves were immortal, right?" asked Bliss. "Romulus was a wolf, yes? Before he was a hound. One of the ancients."

"Yes." Lawson nodded.

"But all the wolves—like you guys—can breed. You can have pups."

"Litters, even," Ahramin added drily. "It's why we're all close in age."

Bliss looked at them, her face flushed with excitement. "I know who the Sabines are."

Lawson looked at her expectantly.

"Only mortals were given the gift of procreation. Vampires cannot procreate, they only reincarnate in new bodies for every cycle. But you can breed, and while you have extraordinary strength and power, you are mortal, which means the ancient wolves—the Praetorian Guard—the Romans—bred with human women. The Sabines are your human mothers."

"And Lucifer ... " Lawson said, his face growing darker.

"Wants to kill you all. He wants to stop wolves from being born. Especially one of you," she said, looking directly at Lawson.

"What?"

"Isn't it clear? He has to stop you from being born. Erase you from the timeline, from history. Lucifer will sacrifice his whole army for it, all his hellhounds, rather than risk the rebellion and the chance that you might live to fight for the other side."

"What are you talking about?"

She was breathless with her own realization.

"You are Fenrir. The great wolf whom legend has foretold will free the wolves from slavery and return them to the glory of the true Praetorian Guard."

There was silence as the group digested this new information. Bliss saw Lawson's brothers look at him in a new light, and even Ahramin was gazing at Lawson with a respectful air.

Lawson frowned and crossed his arms, looking uncomfortable with all the attention. "You don't know that for sure."

"But think about it," she said. "You can enter hallowed ground, and you can make portals through the worlds, something the other wolves can't. And you said so yourself, after your escape there were many others who followed your path to freedom. 'We freed ourselves.' You certainly did. Marrok knew who you were. It was why he encouraged you to escape, why he risked stealing the chronolog. Because it was time. Because you are Fenrir."

"Well then," Malcolm said. "What are we waiting for? Let's go to Rome."

THIRTY-ONE

*L*awson kept his eyes on Bliss as she held the chronolog in one hand and used the other hand to position all the hands on all the faces, lining up the dates and the latitude and longitude positions and then pressing the button on the side of the device. The gears below started to whir and the arms descended onto the points. The device began to buzz, its gears grinding like those of a windup toy.

Entering the timeline felt different from before. The previous trips through the passages had been dizzying, with the bright light rendering Lawson unable to see their movement through history, but now it was as if the chronolog was physically moving him, stopping on occasion in locations that clearly weren't Rome, at least not yet.

One pause: he felt a warm fire at his back and the chill of a winter breeze at his face. Up ahead he saw footprints in the snow. A pair of figures stood in the distance. They wore heavy coats of fur and walked on snowshoes around a circle of tall stones. The image receded. His head ached and his ears felt funny. He turned to Bliss, but before he could speak, the darkness of the passage enveloped them once more as they moved through the timeline.

Another pause: now there was light snow on the ground. They stood in the center of another circle of stones. Beyond the gray monoliths, Lawson saw an earthen mound and a pit. It looked like another portal, another entrance to the passage, just like the serpent mound.

One more: the air darkened, and when they stopped again, Lawson was standing in front of a grouping of stones. They were arranged in long rows. He turned around to see Bliss, Rafe, and Malcolm, who looked dazed. Edon and Ahramin were not far behind.

Lawson tapped Malcolm on the shoulder. "Where are we?"

"I don't know," Malcolm said. "I think we're in France. Maybe Carnac." He placed his hand on the gray stone. Fresh chisel marks littered its rough face.

The light dimmed again, and the darkness returned. Lawson closed his eyes, then opened them to see stars streaking through the black void of the passage. No more pauses now; they were moving quickly through time, through a long patch of nothingness that continued until his whole body ached. He wished for the journey to end, though he knew things would only get harder once they stopped. He clenched his teeth, and his mind lost track of how long they had been traveling.

"It's okay, we're here," he heard a voice say after what seemed an eternity. "Open your eyes."

Lawson felt a warm hand on his back. Bliss. He opened his eyes to a bright Mediterranean sun. In the distance he saw snowcapped mountains stretch downward to a city that was nestled amid seven hills. They were finally in Rome, at the beginning. Red banners stretched from all the buildings; the streets were packed with carts; the buildings' limestone facades shone in the sun. This was the city at its very first breath. This was the dawn of the empire.

They were standing on a third-story balcony overlooking the city. The street below connected to a vast piazza; in the open space a large crowd gathered at the steps of a grand building. At the top of the steps, a red-robed figure, flanked by a group of centurions, waved a golden staff. Everywhere red banners waved in the warm sun as soldiers paraded down the avenue carrying a statue of a ferocious-looking man with a long flowing beard and a trident in one hand.

"Neptune," Malcolm whispered. "You did it. We're here."

"What do we do now, though?" Bliss asked.

"We'll need to blend in," Ahramin said, taking charge. "We can't go out there like this." She indicated their grimy outfits. "Split up—Edon and I will check the lower floor; Mac, you and Rafe check this one. Lawson—you and Bliss whistle if you hear anyone. I think everyone's out at the festival, the place feels empty. I bet not even the servants are around."

Lawson nodded, a bit annoyed that Ahramin was giving orders, but she knew the lay of the land better; as a hound, she had been privy to the old traditions.

He squinted out the window, at the giant robed figure waving his golden staff. Romulus. How strange to think that something that had happened in the past had been caused by an event that was far off in the future. His birth. Was Bliss right? Was he the one? He remembered what Master Corvinus had said—that he was special, that he was to be Romulus's heir. Lucifer had foreseen it himself. The Dark Prince had ordered him turned into a hound before he could fulfill his true destiny.

Everything was hanging in the balance—the past, the future, his life, and the lives of everyone he loved. He didn't want to fail. He thought about the shifting images on the postcard, from kidnapping to murder. History was unfolding before his eyes, and it was his responsibility to make sure the timeline remained intact. He was a wolf, a guardian of the abyss. A keeper of time. He watched Romulus leave the podium, followed by two of his guards. Hounds, most likely. Where was Tala? She had to be close by.

"Someone's coming," Bliss warned.

Lawson nodded, preparing to subdue whoever walked into the room.

"Check me out!" Malcolm said. He was wearing a wool toga with red edging; it was short and sized for a child and the hem didn't come down quite far enough to hide his sneakers. "Nice, right?" The rest of the group were all dressed in similar costume. "We looked out the window, everyone's in red for the parade."

"Here," Edon said, handing folded linens to Lawson and Bliss. "Go and get changed."

When everyone was suitably attired, Lawson called them together and told them how he intended to preserve the timeline. "Remember, everything has to happen the same way. Romulus has to give the signal."

"But the orders from the oculus will tell the hounds to take the women—not kill them," Ahramin said, nodding. "We will take care of it."

Ahramin, Edon, Malcolm, and Rafe left to find the nearest oculus and change the orders. Bliss had opted to stay with Lawson. She was the only one who knew there was more to his plan than simply securing the timeline and saving Tala.

"You don't have to come with me. I can take care of Romulus," he said.

"I know you can. But even Fenrir can use a friend, can't he?"

For once, Lawson did not argue.

THIRTY-TWO

*B*liss followed Lawson through the city. The buildings were cursory structures; the Rome she was familiar with was filled with enormous monuments, basilicas, and temples and palaces, but she reminded herself that they were back at the beginning, before most of those things had been built.

She looked around the plaza, down at the unpaved dirt packed under her feet. The open-air plaza was vast, the crowd overpowering in its size as they waited for the horn that would blow twice to signal the opening of the Consualia, the games that would celebrate Neptune's day. The red banners flapped and cracked in the wind, and the buildings around them were covered in brightly colored paint and graffiti. Splashes of animal blood dripped from the walls into open sewers and there were flies everywhere.

Rome smelled like a corpse. It was a far more vulgar place than she'd imagined. The air was filled with the scent of incense and smoke from burning effigies of Roman gods, mixed with the stink of people sweating in the woolen togas, as she was. She was starting to be able to tell that there were some class distinctions—the wealthier citizens wore togas that appeared to be made of cotton, and accordingly, they looked cooler and more comfortable than everyone else, her included.

Lawson explained that the temple Romulus had been standing in front of was the Regia, the home of kings. They walked toward it quickly, past donkey carts filled with fresh produce, and she plucked a date from an open basket and sunk her teeth into the rich fruit. A man jostled her, and cold wine sloshed from his wooden mug onto her dress.

Everywhere Bliss looked, she saw soldiers like the fierce warriors from her memory. The ancient wolves were magnificent and golden, while the hellhounds, disguised in the same armor they usually wore, were darker and smaller in size and bearing. She almost bumped into one as she made her way deeper into the crowd.

"Sorry," she whispered.

The hound leered at her. He was clearly of a lower order; his armor was made from hardened brown leather, sculpted into the shape of a muscled torso. "Stay a while," he said.

"She's with me," Lawson said.

The soldier spit at the ground but did not fight. Bliss moved nervously away, and Lawson held her hand as they made their way closer to the Regia.

The crowd was edgy and boisterous; it had the air of a mob, restless and eager for trouble. More soldiers were arriving, pouring into the arcades and gathering in groups on the roofs of the crude houses just outside the plaza. The crowd was growing more anxious by the minute. Bliss felt an elbow hit her in the back as two women pushed past her. Another dashed behind them, also elbowing Bliss. The soldiers scanned the crowd with impassive faces.

The games were due to start in moments, at which point the hounds disguised as soldiers would reveal themselves, beginning the slaughter that would end the line of the wolves.

Bliss felt a rough hand on her shoulder. It was the hound she had jostled.

"There you are, pretty." He smiled. "Leave this loser and come with me."

"Leave her alone," Lawson growled.

"Ah—screw you," the hound said. "Romulus said we can take what we can before the signal ..." He pulled on Bliss's toga and tore it from the clasp.

Bliss gasped, held her dress together, and turned to the hound.

"No, it's all right," she told Lawson, who was ready to throw a punch. If he fought the hound, they would start a fight, and the hounds were ready for bloodshed. Ahramin and the boys had to get the orders changed— nothing could happen before then. They couldn't risk the soldiers and the hounds jumping the gun.

She turned to the hound, her eyes boring into its crimson eyes and silver pupils. "You dare threaten me? Do you know who I am?"

The hound looked at her and quivered with fright. "No ... it cannot be ... how is it ..." It backed away, fear in its eyes.

"How do you keep doing that?" Lawson asked when the hound was gone. "Who are you? You have never answered that."

She hesitated as she fixed her strap. Could she lay all her cards on the table? Could she trust him to trust her? "Lawson, at the butcher shop—when I spoke your language ..."

"Yes?"

"You asked how I knew *Hroll*. It was because I saw something in my memory then. I think it was a wolf in his true form. It was an amazing sight. Beautiful." In her mind's eye she could see Lucifer standing at the top of a marble staircase, looking down at the magnificent form of the warrior in front of him. Her father had spoken its language. But now, as Bliss closed her eyes and relived the memory, she saw what happened next, and described it to Lawson.

"I saw Lucifer holding out his hand, and the beautiful warrior fell to his knees. There was a blast of smoke, and when it cleared, the warrior was a wolf, wearing a collar, and his golden eyes were silver."

Lawson stared at her. "What you're describing is the punishment of the wolves," he said. "How could you have seen this?"

Bliss shook her head slowly. She wasn't sure if it was the right time to tell Lawson the truth; she had no idea how he would react. And they had so much ahead of them, so much to do. But she didn't want to keep the secret any longer. "Because it's not only my mother's memories I share. I share my father's memories as well. I had access to his mind once, and he was part of mine."

"Your father?"

She flinched. "My father ... was Lucifer," she whispered. "I am the daughter of the Dark Prince of Hell. I was kept alive, hidden by his loyal followers, reincarnated through the centuries, to keep his spirit alive on earth. I did not know. He used me as a vessel for his evil. I have his memories and I am his flesh and blood."

For a long time, nothing happened. Lawson didn't speak. Bliss was worried he was trying to figure out a way to kill her in public, without anyone noticing. But when she finally dared to look at him, he didn't seem angry. Only contemplative.

"So you're not just an ex-vampire," he finally said.

"No." She could see the wheels in his mind turning. He was putting all the pieces together.

"The hounds know," he said. "They sense it, they sense that you carry the blood of the Dark Prince himself. It frightens them away."

"I'm sorry I didn't tell you sooner. And I'm sorry for what my father did to your people. But I'm not him. I don't want any part of him."

"You *are* part of him, though," he said, and finally there was the anger that she had expected.

"That sword that you have ... I used to kill his spirit inside me. I wanted to die rather than live with what I had done. Please," she said. "Please believe me. Look."

She pulled down her neckline to show part of the scar across her torso, right across her heart. "That's all that's left. I'm not lying. I thought I would die, but instead I became mortal."

"We owe you a debt, without your memories, we would never have been able to use the chronolog. But after this is over . . . we will part ways. The wolves owe no debt to the vampires. We will fight no demons in your name. Now leave me, for I have no wish for your company. I have a hound to kill."

here were tears in her eyes when she turned away from him, but Lawson hardened his heart, even though the sight of the vicious scar on her chest had given him pause. She was a distraction; he was here to kill Romulus and save Tala; he couldn't spare a moment to think of Bliss. If she was working with the enemy, then it was better that he had sent her away. If she was who she said she was, an ex-vampire, an archangel's daughter, then she would still be safe. The hounds would not harm her; he saw that much.

The crowd was restless for the games to begin, but he knew they had some time; only Romulus could signal the opening of the games, and Romulus had not yet returned to the balcony. Lawson planned to find Tala first, then kill the general only after Romulus had given the signal. History must be allowed to flow as it had. At the steps of the Regia, he tried to sniff out Tala's scent, but the smell of the hounds masked everything else, the stench of their evil filling the air.

The Regia was enormous, easily the largest of the surrounding buildings. Lawson evaded the guards watching the steps and slipped into the main chamber, unsure which of the numerous corridors to follow. Where would Romulus keep Tala? Lawson would have expected that he'd keep her by his side, but he hadn't seen her on the podium with Romulus when he stood before the crowd. She must be here. But where?

Lawson began exploring the palace. He wandered through room after room on the first floor. The dining room, filled with recliners for royalty to lie on during their meals. No chairs for the elite, not in ancient Rome. Some of the recliners were clearly meant for one person; others were semicircular and could seat a number of people. An interior kitchen, with a fire pit for roasting meat and long tables and serving stands. Bedroom after bedroom, with sleeping couches holding high, fluffy feather beds, covered in blankets and pillows. If Romulus was keeping her by his side, then she'd be in a room closer to Romulus's chambers, or even in his chambers themselves. The thought twisted his stomach, but he had to keep going.

Corridor after corridor, room after room. Finally, he saw a door that bore the sigil of the republic. Romulus's quarters. She had to be in there. *Tala, where are you?*

The bedroom was larger and more elaborate than any he'd seen so far. The bed was enormous, the mattress higher off the ground than any of the others. Lawson sat down and sunk deeply into the plush feather bed. Apparently firm mattresses were a thing of the future, he thought. He tried to picture Tala here, to pick up her scent. Nothing.

He heaved himself off the tall bed and explored the rest of the room. Wooden shelves held togas, spare armor, leather sandals. The togas were lighter and softer than the one he wore, some made of cotton, some of silk. Too bad there weren't any extra weapons lying around. No sign that a woman had been here; none of the tunics looked like dresses, like the ones Bliss and Ahramin were wearing.

Except . . .

He turned his head to the corner of the bedroom. There was a pile of what appeared to be laundry sitting in the corner. Funny how some things stayed the same, no matter what century you were in, he thought; people still left their clothes on the floor. But then he looked closer. The clothes appeared to be silk; they glistened as he moved toward them. He picked up the fabric and saw that it was a woman's tunic, soft to the touch and beautifully cut, as best as he could tell.

And covered in bloodstains.

Lawson felt as if he couldn't breathe. *Tala . . . where are you? What happened here?*

It couldn't be hers, could it? But it had to be. Romulus had taken no mate, and he'd shown himself to be insistent on doing whatever he could to destroy Lawson, to destroy whatever power he thought Lawson possessed. He didn't want to think about what Romulus had done to her, about the prospect of never seeing Tala again. It couldn't be true.

"She's not here, my boy."

Lawson turned around to see Romulus standing at the doorway.

THIRTY-FOUR

Bliss stumbled into the crowd blindly, blinking back tears, not caring where she was going, not knowing what to do, or what to think. She had trusted him to accept her as she was, and he had rejected her. She could still see the hate that had been in his eyes when she'd told him—but what did she expect? Of course he would react that way—her father had cursed his people, turned them into beasts, made them slaves. How could he see past that? She barreled through the crowd, unseeing, until by accident she bumped into Rafe.

"Bliss!" he cried.

"What's wrong? What happened?" she asked. "Why aren't you at the oculus?"

"Ahramin sent me to find you. The oculus does not

respond. We cannot change the order. She thinks the masters have locked it off somehow, to keep anyone from tampering with it. Where's Lawson?"

Bliss shook her head. "We don't need Lawson right now." Lawson might have dismissed her, but Bliss knew what she had to do. Lawson had sent the wrong person to the oculus. She was of the same blood as the masters, and because she was Lucifer's daughter, the hounds would follow her every command. Only she could stop the massacre. "Take me to the oculus, quickly."

The oculus was housed in the great Temple of Mars, and when Bliss arrived, Ahramin and the boys had managed to clear the area; the hellhound guards were dead or subdued, bound with silver chains. There was no time to explain, and Bliss stepped directly into the light of the oculus in the center of the room.

It was like being in the passages; it was all connected, she realized, the oculi, the dark roads, all part of the great network of space and time. Bliss stepped inside the abyss and sent out the message, seeing each hound in the light, their souls as dark stars in the firmament.

You shall not harm the Sabine women but take them as wives. The Dark Prince himself wishes this so.

One by one the light of each hound brightened in

response. The message was being received and transmitted to the hive mind.

Bliss hesitated—she realized the oculus could help her in another way. "Show me the Watcher," she ordered.

The images whirred and flew, and finally she saw her aunt. Jane Murray was wearing a raincoat and walking purposefully through a gray, foggy city. She was alive and unharmed. Bliss called to her through the vortex of space and time.

When Bliss stepped out of the oculus, Ahramin was waiting. "We saw the light flash, it meant the message went out. You are one of them," the dark girl said. "Lucifer's kin."

Bliss did not argue. She looked at the boys, worried about their reaction. "I am sorry that I did not tell you sooner, but while I am my father's daughter, I am my own person. He is as much my enemy as yours."

"You don't need to explain," Malcolm said, and hugged her. "You saved the timeline."

"Where is Lawson? Does he know about you?" Ahramin asked.

She nodded. "Yes," she said, not wanting to share any more information for now.

They heard footsteps from the entrance to the temple.

Ahramin turned to the boys. "Guard this place. Make sure no one else uses the oculus. Bliss and I will go to Lawson. Come," she said to Bliss, moving her away from the brothers.

"Look, Lawson doesn't want me around, I'll stay here," Bliss said.

Ahramin shook her head. "There is no time to be bashful. Listen, Lawson thinks he can kill Romulus with the archangel's sword."

Bliss nodded.

"He can't."

"Why not?"

"Because I stole it," Ahramin said, trembling. "When I shook his hand, when he released me." She showed Bliss the velvet pouch that contained Michael's sword. "I've had it ever since."

Bliss stared at her. "You sent him to his death! Romulus will destroy him! What were you thinking!" Then she realized. "You lied to us. You are still a Hound of Hell."

Ahramin's body was wracked with spasms. "I tried to fight it—Romulus left me in the house as bait—he hoped that somehow Lawson would find out—and come back for me. I was supposed to deliver them all to him—but I fought it, as long as I could."

Bliss stared at the shaking girl, seeing the broken patient from the hospital again. "Your cough. Your body was fighting your will."

"Yes."

"But hallowed ground—how did you manage it? I thought hounds weren't allowed to be in those places."

"St. Bernadette's was not holy. It was once run by an order, but it is a public hospital now. I made sure before they took me there."

"Why are you telling me this now?"

"I have fought the collar as much as I could, but it is killing me. With every step I take to help the wolves, it takes another piece of my soul. I am going to die now," Ahramin said. "But I don't want . . . I don't want *them* to die." She motioned to the temple, where the boys were fighting the hounds. "Edon doesn't know. I don't want him to know I was ever false. Please, let him still love me, even when I am gone."

"Why should I believe anything you say?"

"Because you love Lawson and you want to help him. I love him too. Will you help me?"

THIRTY-FIVE

*I*n human form, Romulus was an enormous man, nearly seven feet in height. His shadow covered Lawson, his blinding red robe fluttering in an iridescent halo around him. No simple togas for him, silk or otherwise; he was arrayed in full golden battle armor, with the sweeping robe flowing from his shoulders. In one hand he carried the golden staff Lawson had seen from the window, a weapon as heavy as a pair of Roman soldiers. A red fire roared in his black eyes as he smiled at Lawson, a strange, eerie smile.

"Where is she?" Lawson asked. "Where's Tala?"

Romulus laughed. "Where do you think she is? She's dead, of course."

"You're lying." Lawson tapped his pocket, looking for

the sword he had stolen from the underworld, the sword of the angels, but it was nowhere to be found.

Romulus smiled as he smacked him down with his golden staff, felling him as easily as if he were a child or a small animal. An annoyance, nothing more. Lawson fell backward on the hard stone. He heard his skull crack, blood trailing from the wound.

What had happened . . . ?

Where was the sword?

Bliss?

Had she . . . ?

The heavy staff came down again and again, and he collapsed against the force of more blows from Romulus. He held up his hands to shield his face, but a silver claw embedded at the top of the golden scepter cut deep into his chest.

Lawson tried to lift himself off the floor and Romulus clubbed him in the back with a blow so powerful it might have cleaved a normal man in half. The Great Beast of Hell hovered over him. "Silly boy," the general said. "You should have joined us when we still wanted you. Instead, you doomed her to her fate."

"You didn't need to kill her. What harm was she to you alive?"

"She was useful for a time," Romulus said, and

Lawson didn't want to think what the flicker in the fire of his eyes meant. "A pity she wasn't any prettier, though. Otherwise I might have kept her around a bit longer."

Lawson groaned. He looked over at the bloody toga, just feet away from where he lay on the ground. Tala was here, but he had come too late.

Romulus laughed. "Oh, that thing? No, you're mistaken. That was not hers."

Lawson felt a surge of hope.

"When you left her to burn in that house, I killed her myself. Besides, why keep her alive when I could gain the same advantage by having Ahramin tell you a lie? Your mate has been dead for a very long time now. Truly, you should have listened to your brothers and kept moving. But when you showed yourself at the oculus, it was clear you still had hope, just like you had only a moment ago, when I told you the clothes weren't hers. It gives me great pleasure to watch that hope die, the hope that is your downfall."

Lawson writhed on the floor, holding his head. He was bleeding from his wounds—and the silver poison was working its way into his blood. He would die. But it didn't matter.

Tala was dead.

She'd been dead from the beginning.

She'd been dead since he'd left her. She was dead . . .

Tala . . .

It was all a dream, this idea that he could rescue her, a stupid dream. A fantasy. His guilt had prodded him on because he hadn't wanted to accept what had happened. He'd known she was as good as dead when he left her to the hounds, but he wouldn't accept it. He knew, but if he accepted it, he'd also have to accept that she'd been killed because of him, because of who he was, what he was.

Tala had pushed him away. She knew what was going to happen. She knew that if they left her behind, the hounds would come and tear her apart. But she loved him, so she had saved him.

Tala, I've failed you . . . and now I've failed everyone . . .

"*Fenrir,*" Romulus sneered. "The great hope of the wolves. The man out of time, whom time cannot hold. The one who would save them all, who would free them from their chains. I gave you a choice back then to join me, and you chose unwisely. There will be no freedom for the wolves. After today, there will be no wolves at all."

Romulus moved to the balcony and gave the signal to commence the attack.

THIRTY-SIX

"Something's wrong," Romulus growled; he moved away from the balcony. Bleeding from his wounds on the floor, Lawson could hear the sounds of screaming and chaos, but if Romulus was not satisfied, then maybe, just maybe, his pack had succeeded in changing the orders. Maybe it meant the Sabines would survive, and so would the line of wolves.

The great general turned to him with a menacing glare. "This is your doing," he hissed. "There is no other way. The orders were clear."

Lawson managed a weak laugh; if this was all the victory he would taste, he would savor it before the end. "It is too late ... you will not be able to change it ... "

"No matter," Romulus said. "You were the gravest

threat to the Dark Prince and you will die today." Once again, he struck Lawson with the staff, sending him skittering to the far wall.

Lawson was too debilitated by his injuries to protect himself but he did not care. He would die, but he had saved the wolves. Bliss was wrong; he was no Fenrir, but maybe Marrok would find a way to bring them out of the underworld.

Romulus raised his staff again, but a voice rang from the balcony.

"Don't touch him. You are nothing but my father's dog," Bliss said, entering the room. She must have climbed up from the back way to avoid being seen, Lawson thought. But what was she doing here? Why had she returned? Why did she care? Wasn't she the one who had stolen the angel's sword from him?

"Ah, Lucifer's bastard. He has been searching for you," Romulus said, smiling. "Why don't you return to him? Do not waste your time with this filth."

Bliss smiled. "I have a message you can send to my father ... Ahri, now!" she said as she tossed Michael's sword to Lawson. The archangel's blade glinted golden in the sunlight while Ahramin stepped out of the shadows. She was wearing thick black gloves and holding a heavy silver chain.

"Stay, hound. You are still one of mine. I can hear your thoughts as clearly as I hear my own. You are correct in believing you will die if you do not listen to me," Romulus said.

With a great scream, Ahramin leapt and wrapped the chain twice around Romulus's neck, climbing on his back as she pulled and tightened, and the Great Beast of Hell fell to his knees.

"Remove it! If you treasure your life, you will do as I say!" Romulus ordered as he struggled with the chain, which smoked around his skin. As powerful as he was, he was still a creature of Hell, and silver was poison to him as well.

The scars on Ahramin's neck began to throb, and a silver collar appeared against the skin as Romulus bent his will to hers. She wrestled and thrashed against it, howling in pain, but slowly, excruciatingly, she began to remove the silver chain around Romulus's neck. "I'm so sorry ... " She sobbed. "I'm so sorry, I can't fight him anymore ... "

They were losing time. "Lawson!" Bliss yelled. "Do it!"

With a roar, Romulus threw Ahramin off his back, and he turned to pick up his staff. Romulus snarled and readied to launch the final blow.

But Lawson had gotten up. If he could stand, he

could fight, and if he could fight, he could hold a sword. He felt the weight of it in his palm, and he stood, uncertainly. He was broken and battered but he was resolute.

"For Tala," he whispered. "For all the wolves in the underworld." Then he lunged with the blade, which cut through the golden armor like butter, and he stuck it deep into Romulus's black heart.

The Great Beast of Hell howled in pain, and his whole body began to shift, from wolf to man and back, trembling and shaking and smoking, until finally only a small black wolf lay dead on the floor before it disappeared in dark smoke.

There was a clamor and the rest of the pack entered the room. Rafe and Malcolm ran to Lawson, Malcolm's eyes wide with fright, but Edon had eyes for only one person.

"Ahri!" Edon yelled, running to her side; she lay still on the ground next to Romulus. He knelt and cradled her in his arms. "Don't leave me. Don't leave me."

She was lifeless in his arms, and the silver collar was still around her neck, but when Romulus's heart exploded, the collar fell apart and broke in two.

Finally, she opened her eyes. "I told you, there is still wolf in me." She smiled, and Edon kissed her.

*

Lawson collapsed to the floor even as his wounds began to heal. The silver poison had disappeared with Romulus's death. He put his sword away as he turned to Bliss. "I'm sorry I doubted you," he said as she knelt down to hear him.

"Never mind that now, did you find Tala?" she asked.

He shook his head to indicate no hope remained, but he had little time to dwell on that for now. "What about your aunt Jane?" he asked.

"She got away. I asked the oculus to show her to me, when I changed the orders. She told me she led the hounds through the passages but she was able to slip away at the very end. She went to London, she said. She told me to meet her there. The Blue Bloods need us there."

Lawson removed the postcard he kept in his pocket and turned it over to read the text: *The Abduction of the Sabines*. They had succeeded in keeping the timeline safe, in killing Romulus. The wolves would soon be free, and there was still hope for the hounds as well; Ahramin had shown that. Lawson should have felt joy, but all he felt was exhaustion.

"I'm sorry about Tala," Bliss said, and squeezed his hand. "I wish it had been otherwise."

He had won, and yet he had lost. Bliss, of all people, seemed to understand that victory and triumph were not the same.

THIRTY-SEVEN

*T*he chronolog took them back through time, and as they moved through the passages, Lawson could see places that looked familiar. The monastery, in Venice. France, with the enormous carved stones. He stopped in front of a house that looked more familiar than most.

"I'm sorry, I thought we were going back to the serpent mound," Bliss said. "But this thing seems to have a mind of its own."

Lawson looked at the structure in front of them. It was half-built, with only the foundation and the wood frame. He hadn't recognized it at first, but now he did. "Can you take us here, only closer to the present? A week before we met?"

"I can help," Malcolm said, and showed Bliss how to set the chronolog again.

Again they moved through time, but more quickly. Probably because they didn't have far to go, Lawson figured. The passages finally landed them where he wanted to be.

"Where are we?" Bliss asked. "Is this where we're supposed to go?"

"That's the house," he said, pointing to an ordinary-looking brown house at the end of a familiar cul-de-sac. There was a foreclosure sign on the front lawn. "Look, we'd just arrived, the curtains aren't up yet. Remember those, Mac?"

"I remember," Malcolm said quietly.

"Lawson, we need to keep moving," Bliss said. "Marrok might need our help."

"Hold on just a moment," he said excitedly. "See, we can change what happened. I can leave a message— tell them to run. Tell myself to run. So they won't stay here. Then the hounds won't come and Tala will be alive. She'll be *alive*." Lawson turned to them, his eyes shining.

But his brothers just shook their heads. Ahramin was mute, hesitant.

"Bliss . . . you understand, help me. Help me do this."

"No, Lawson." Her tone was kind, but firm. "You know the rules. You're a Praetorian. You can't change the past. You can't change what's happened. Time must be allowed to flow, and the course of history must remain unchanged. You told me that."

"No, not in this instance. No."

"You've got to let her go, Lawson. It's the only way you're going to be able to move forward," Bliss said. She put a hand on his arm. "I know you loved her, but you've got to say goodbye."

Lawson closed his eyes. Bliss was right. Of course she was right. He couldn't change what had happened, not if he wanted to remain true to what he was, to what Tala had loved about him from the start.

With tears in his eyes, he watched as the door opened and Tala appeared in the doorway. He felt his heart swell with love and sadness.

Tala looked across the way, almost as if she were looking right at him, but he knew she couldn't see him.

She had a smile on her face. She was happy. They'd been happy for a while in that little brown house. A bright and peaceful happiness after the darkness of their life in the underworld. It hadn't lasted very long, but Lawson would treasure that love; he wouldn't let his love destroy him. He would let it make him stronger.

Tala.

She was so beautiful and kind. She loved him so much.

Every moment in time happened all at the same moment. That was the way of it in the Passages of Time. There was no past and no future, only an endless present. And in this moment, Tala was alive, and Tala was happy. He would have this moment forever, he realized. It was not lost; he could return to it, again and again, in his memory. It would sustain him. He thought of Bliss, who had suffered a loss as well. *I lost someone too, and he's gone,* she'd said. *I have to let go.* He would be strong for her, he thought. He would move on, like she had.

Tala, I love you. Goodbye.

Why, Lawson, where are you going?

He recoiled. She had heard him. She looked out into the darkness with a frown on her face. Then she turned around and there he was. The Lawson from the past was standing behind her. He put his arms around her and they kissed.

Lawson remembered that kiss.

It had been a good one.

"Lawson, we've set the coordinates," Bliss said. "We're ready to go."

He turned away from the house and followed his pack down the passage.

THIRTY-EIGHT

This time they landed in the dark, underground, deep within the earth. "We must be under the serpent mound," Malcolm said.

"Start walking," Rafe said.

Lawson led the group through the narrow tunnels, limping a little. Finally they reached the end of the tunnel; the sun lit the exit, and they rose out of the ground, one by one, until they were all standing next to the serpent mound. Lawson signaled the team to remain behind him. He looked down at the ground. It was covered in blood, a dark red stain on the dirt and grass.

"Marrok?" he whispered.

What had happened here? He felt a sickening lurch in

his stomach, a knot of guilt forming at the thought of what he'd left the wolves behind to do.

"Hounds?" Bliss asked.

Malcolm shook his head. "I think they're gone," he said. "I feel fine."

Rain began to fall, lightly, in cold drops. The sun remained in the sky but its light faded, though not enough to block the sight of a body, just steps past the entrance. It was Ulric, the big wolf. He'd been gutted from belly to throat. It made sense that he would have been the last to fall; Lawson remembered from the pits he'd been a fierce warrior. It appeared the wolves had held off the hounds as long as they could, but ultimately they had lost. The field was strewn with the corpses of dead wolves, some in human form, some in their wolf skin. There were dead hounds too; Lawson noted with satisfaction that the wolves had taken down many of them, more than he'd expected them to.

"Ulf," a voice called.

Lawson saw Marrok lying motionless in the damp earth. A black sword was wedged in his chest. The rain had begun to wash the wound clear, but Marrok had lacked the strength to remove it. The metal glistened in the faint sunlight.

Lawson removed the blade. Marrok began to heave

with pain. The rain grew stronger and poured over his face, welling in his eyes and nostrils. His skin was pale and still, almost lifeless. Lawson pressed a firm hand to the cut and dark blood flowed outward through his fingers. He said the words that Arthur had taught him, and prayed that Marrok would heal.

"It's no use," the fallen wolf said. "The hounds' swords carry the Black Fire. Nothing can help me now."

"Marrok . . . brother . . . " Lawson said, feeling tears form in his eyes.

"We held them off as long as we could," Marrok said.

"You fought bravely," Lawson said, and everyone else nodded behind him. "It was not in vain. We made it to Rome and averted the massacre. The timeline is intact. Romulus is dead. The Great Beast of Hell has been silenced."

Marrok smiled and coughed; dark blood dribbled from his chin.

"What can I do for you, my brother?" Lawson asked. "How can I ease your passage?"

Marrok closed his eyes, and Lawson was afraid he had already lost him. Then, with some effort, he opened them again. "Promise me again what we promised back in the underworld. That you will free all of our people, that you will not rest until we return to our former glory, as guardians of the abyss. Use your power to restore order and keep the timeline pure. Now that the passages are open, time is vulnerable. You must guard them, protect against their misuse. It is imperative that they do not fall into the wrong hands. Even as Romulus has been defeated, there are others who will use the passages for their own gain. The Dark Prince ... "

"You have my word," Lawson said, clasping his hand.

They sat there together for a long time, long enough that Lawson thought maybe Marrok had been wrong, maybe there was a chance that he could make it. The rain continued to fall, washing the dirt from Marrok's white hair, mixing with the tears now streaming from Lawson's eyes.

Edon, Malcolm, Rafe, and Ahramin all knelt down on the muddy ground, encircling the fallen wolf. Bliss knelt with them, next to Lawson, pushing his wet hair off his forehead and then placing her hand on his back. The feel of her palm steadied him as he watched Marrok fighting the pain. Was it possible? Was there any hope?

Marrok lifted his head to look Lawson in the eye. "It's been an honor, Fenrir," he whispered. Then he closed his eyes. His skin went gray, then black as the fire of Hell consumed him.

"Goodbye, my friend," Lawson said.

Lawson regarded his pack. His brothers: Malcolm, Rafe, Edon. Ahramin, who had returned to them. Bliss, the vampire in their midst. He turned to her now. "The Fallen need us for this task, you say. To help them in this war against our masters."

"Yes."

He nodded. "We will go with you. We will help you," he said. He had meant what he'd said; he should never have doubted her for a moment, regardless of her parentage. Bliss Llewellyn was his friend. Maybe more, if he would let her be. It was too soon to think of that now. His feelings were too new, too painful after discovering what had happened to Tala. He thought of what the oculus had shown him. He had asked it to show him his mate, and he had seen Bliss in the light. Did they have a future together?

"You have a wolf's name, and like us, you are a creature of the underworld. If you take the pact, you will be one of us," he said.

"I'll say the words, if you will lead," she said softly.

Together they formed a circle and began to recite the words that bound them to each other.

We are wolves of the guard, soldiers of the light.
Hunted and haunted, by the beasts of the night.
Friend to all and foe to none,
Love and loyalty bind us as one.
Time and tide shall heal all wounds
Memories and madness shall not consume.
To death and despair we shall never surrender,
The pact never to be forsaken, or torn asunder.

Lawson laid a hand on Bliss's cheek. When he removed it, her skin glowed with a pale blue crescent sign.

He turned to the other girl. His onetime rival, his onetime alpha. "Ahramin, you have returned to us, and we accept you as our sister once again."

"I am proud to run with you once more," Ahramin said. She felt her cheek in wonderment. "My sigil—it's returned," she whispered.

Then slowly, one by one, the six wolves walked back into the forest.

Turn the page
for an extract from

Blue Bloods

the book that began it all

The Bank was a decrepit stone building at the tail end of Houston Street, on the last divide between the gritty East Village and the wilds of the Lower East Side. Once the headquarters of the venerable Van Alen investment and brokerage house, it was an imposing, squat presence, a paradigm of the beaux-arts style, with a classic six-column façade and an intimidating row of "dentals"—razor-sharp serrations on the pediment's surface. For many years it stood on the corner of Houston and Essex, desolate, empty, and abandoned, until one winter evening when an eye-patch-wearing nightclub promoter chanced upon it after polishing off a hot dog at Katz's Deli. He was looking for a venue to showcase the new music his DJs were spinning—a dark, haunted sound they were calling "Trance."

The pulsing music spilled out to the sidewalk, where Schuyler Van Alen, a small, dark-haired fifteen-year-old girl, whose bright blue eyes were ringed with dark kohl eye shadow, stood nervously at the back of the line in front of the club. She picked at her chipping black nail polish. "Do you really think we'll get in?" she asked.

"No sweat," her best friend, Oliver Hazard-Perry replied, cocking an eyebrow. "Dylan guaranteed a cakewalk. Besides, we can always point to the plaque over there. Your family built this place, remember?" He grinned.

"So what else is new?" Schuyler smirked, rolling her eyes. The island of Manhattan was linked inexorably to her family history, and as far as she could tell, she was related to the Frick Museum, the Van Wyck Expressway, and the Hayden Planetarium, give or take an institution (or major thoroughfare) or two. Not that it made any difference in her life. She barely had enough to cover the twenty-five dollar charge at the door.

Oliver affectionately swung an arm around her shoulders. "Stop worrying! You worry too much. This'll be fun, I promise."

"I wish Dylan had waited for us," Schuyler fretted,

shivering in her long black cardigan with holes in each elbow. She'd found the sweater in a Manhattan Valley thrift store last week. It smelled like decay and stale rose-water perfume, and her skinny frame was lost in its voluminous folds. Schuyler always looked like she was drowning in fabric. The black sweater reached almost to her calves, and underneath she wore a sheer black T-shirt over a worn gray thermal undershirt; and under that, a long peasant skirt that swept the floor. Like a nineteenth century street urchin, her skirt hems were black with dirt from dragging on the sidewalks. She was wearing her favorite pair of black-and-white Jack Purcell sneakers, the ones with the duct-taped hole on the right toe. Her dark wavy hair was pulled back with a beaded scarf she'd found in her grandmother's closet.

Schuyler was startlingly pretty, with a sweet, heart-shaped face; a perfectly upturned nose; and soft, milky skin—but there was something almost insubstantial about her beauty. She looked like a Dresden doll in witch's cloth-ing. Kids at the Duchesne School thought she dressed like a bag lady. It didn't help that she was painfully shy and kept to herself, because then they just thought she was stuck-up, which she wasn't. She was just quiet.

Oliver was tall and slim, with a fair, elfin face that was framed by a shag of brilliant chestnut hair. He had sharp cheekbones and sympathetic hazel eyes. He was wearing a severe military greatcoat over a flannel shirt and a pair of holey blue jeans. Of course, the flannel shirt was John Varvatos and the jeans from Citizens of Humanity. Oliver liked to play the part of disaffected youth, but he liked shopping in SoHo even more.

The two of them had been best friends ever since the second grade, when Schuyler's nanny forgot to pack her lunch one day, and Oliver had given her half of his lettuce and mayo sandwich. They finished each other's sentences and liked to read aloud from random pages of *Infinite Jest* when they were bored. Both were Duchesne legacy kids who traced their ancestry back to the *Mayflower*. Schuyler counted six U.S. presidents in her family tree alone. But even with their prestigious pedigrees, they didn't fit in at Duchesne. Oliver preferred museums to lacrosse, and Schuyler never cut her hair and wore things from consignment shops.

Dylan Ward was a new friend—a sad-faced boy with long lashes, smoldering eyes, and a tarnished reputation. Supposedly, he had a rap sheet and had just been sprung from military school. His grandfather had reportedly bribed Duchesne with funds for a new gym to let him enroll. He had immediately gravitated toward Schuyler and Oliver, recognizing their similar misfit status.

Schuyler sucked in her cheeks and felt a pit of anxiety forming in her stomach. They'd been so comfortable just hanging out in Oliver's room as usual, listening to music and flipping through the offerings on his TiVo; Oliver booting up another game of Vice City on the split screen, while she rifled through the pages of glossy magazines, fantasizing that she too, was lounging on a raft in Sardinia, dancing the flamenco in Madrid, or wandering pensively through the streets of Bombay.

"I'm not sure about this," she said, wishing they were back in his cozy room instead of shivering outside on the sidewalk, waiting to see if they would pass muster at the door.

"Don't be so negative," Oliver chastised. It had been his idea to leave the comfort of his room to brave the New York nightlife, and he didn't want to regret it. "If you think we'll get in, we'll get in. It's all about confidence, trust me." Just then, his BlackBerry beeped. He pulled it out of his pocket and checked the screen. "It's Dylan. He's inside, he'll meet us by the windows on the second floor. Okay?"

"Do I really look all right?" she asked, feeling suddenly doubtful about her clothes.

"You look fine," he replied automatically. "You look

great," he said, as his thumbs jabbed a reply on the plastic device.

"You're not even looking at me."

"I look at you every day." Oliver laughed, meeting her eye, then uncharacteristically blushing and looking away. His BlackBerry beeped again, and this time he excused himself, walking away to answer it.

Across the street, Schuyler saw a cab pull up to the curb, and a tall blond guy stepped out of it. Just as he emerged, another cab barreled down the street on the opposite side. It was swerving recklessly, and at first it looked like it would miss him, but at the last moment, the boy threw himself in its path and disappeared underneath its wheels. The taxicab never even stopped, just kept going as if nothing happened.

"Oh my God!" Schuyler screamed.

The guy had been hit—she was sure of it—he'd been run over—he was surely dead.

"Did you see that?" she asked, frantically looking around for Oliver, who seemed to have disappeared. Schuyler ran across the street, fully expecting to see a dead body, but the boy was standing right in front of her, counting the change in his wallet. He slammed the door shut and sent his taxi on its way. He was whole and unhurt.

"You should be dead," she whispered.

"Excuse me?" he asked, a quizzical smile on his face.

Schuyler was a little taken aback—she recognized him from school. It was Jack Force. The famous Jack Force. One of those guys—head of the lacrosse team, lead in the school play, his term paper on shopping malls published in *Wired*, so handsome she couldn't even meet his eye.

Maybe she was dreaming things. Maybe she just *thought* she'd seen him dive in front of the cab. That had to be it. She was just tired.

"I didn't know you were a dazehead," she blurted awkwardly, meaning a Trance acolyte.

"I'm not, actually. I'm headed over there," he explained, motioning to the club next door to The Bank, where a very intoxicated rock star was steering several giggling groupies past the velvet rope.

Schuyler blushed. "Oh, I should have known."

He smiled at her kindly. "Why?"

"Why what?"

"Why apologize? How would you have known that? You read minds or something?" he asked.

"Maybe I do. And maybe it's an off day." She smiled. He was flirting with her, and she was flirting back. Okay, so it was definitely just her imagination. He had totally not thrown himself in front of the cab.

She was surprised he was being so friendly. Most of the guys at Duchesne were so stuck-up, Schuyler didn't bother with them. They were all the same—with their Duck Head chinos and their guarded nonchalance, their bland jokes and their lacrosse field jackets. She'd never given Jack Force more than a fleeting thought— he was a junior, from the planet Popular; they might go to the same school but they hardly breathed the same air. And after all, his twin sister was the indomitable Mimi Force, whose one goal in life was to make everyone else's miserable. "On your way to a funeral?" "Who died and made you homeless?" were some of Mimi's unimaginative insults directed her way. Where was Mimi, anyway? Weren't the Force twins joined at the hip?

"Listen, you want to come in?" Jack asked, smiling and showing his even, straight teeth. "I'm a member."

Before she could respond, Oliver materialized at her side. Where had he come from? Schuyler wondered. And how did he keep doing that? Oliver demonstrated a keen ability to suddenly show up the minute you didn't want him there. "There you are, my dear," he said, with a hint of reproach.

Schuyler blinked. "Hey, Ollie. Do you know Jack?"

"Who doesn't?" Oliver replied, pointedly ignoring him. "Babe, you coming?" he demanded in a proprietary tone. "They're finally letting people in." He motioned to The Bank, where a steady stream of black-clad teenagers were being herded through the fluted columns.

"I should go," she said apologetically.

"So soon?" Jack asked, his eyes dancing again.

"Not soon enough," Oliver added, smiling threateningly.

Jack shrugged. "See you around, Schuyler," he said, pulling up the collar on his tweed coat and walking in the opposite direction.

"Some people," Oliver complained, as they rejoined their line. He crossed his arms and looked annoyed.

Schuyler was silent, her heart fluttering in her chest.

Jack Force knew her name.

They inched forward, ever closer to the drag queen with the clipboard glaring imperiously behind the velvet rope. The Elvira clone sized up each group with a withering stare, but no one was turned away.

"Now, remember, if they give us any trouble, just be cool and think positive. You have to visualize us getting in, okay?" Oliver whispered fiercely.

Schuyler nodded. They walked forward, but their progress was interrupted by a bouncer holding up a big meaty paw. "IDs!" he barked.

With shaking fingers, Schuyler retrieved a driver's license with someone else's name—but her own picture—on its laminated surface. Oliver did the same. She bit her lip. She was *so* going to get caught and thrown in jail for this. But she remembered what Oliver had said. *Be cool. Confident. Think positive.*

The bouncer waved their IDs under an infrared machine, which didn't beep. He paused, frowning, and held their IDs up for inspection, giving the two of them a doubtful look.

Schuyler tried to project a calm she didn't feel, her heart beating fast underneath her thin layers. Of course I look twenty-one. I've been here before. There is absolutely nothing wrong with that ID, she thought.

The bouncer slid it under the machine again. The big man shook his head. "This isn't right," he muttered.

Oliver looked at Schuyler, his face pale. Schuyler thought she was going to faint. She had never been so nervous in her life. Minutes ticked by. People behind them in line made impatient noises.

Nothing wrong with that ID. Cool and confident. Cool and confident. She visualized the bouncer waving them through, the two of them entering the club. *LET US IN. LET US IN. LET US IN. JUST LET US IN!*

The bouncer looked up, startled, almost as if he'd heard her. It felt as though time had stopped. Then, just like that, he returned their cards and waved them forward, just as Schuyler had pictured.

Schuyler exhaled. She and Oliver exchanged a restrained look of glee.

They were inside.

TWO

*R*ight next door to The Bank was a very different kind of Manhattan nightclub. It was the
kind of nightclub that existed only once every decade—
at a point in the social nexus when the gods of publicity,
fashion, and celebrity converged to create a singularly
spectacular environment. Following in the hallowed tradition of mid-'70s Studio 54, late-'80s Palladium, and
early-'90s Moomba, Block 122 had entered an iconic
realm that defined a movement, a lifestyle, a generation.
A cocktail-combo clientele of the city's most beautiful,
envied, notorious, and all-powerful citizens had chris-
tened it their place to be—their natural habitat, their
watering hole—and since it was the twenty-first century,
the era of super-exclusivity, they even paid astronomical

membership dues for the privilege. Anything to keep out the hoi polloi. And inside this blessed sanctuary, at the most sought-after table, surrounded by a glittering assortment of underage models, post-pubescent movie stars, and the sons and daughters of boldfaced names, sat the most gorgeous girl in the history of New York City: Madeleine "Mimi" Force. Sixteen years old going on thirty-four, with a shot of Botox between the eyes to prove it.

Mimi was popularity personified. She had the golden-girl good looks and tanned, Pilates-toned limbs that came with the Queen Bee position—but she transcended the stereotype while embodying the essence of it. She had a size twenty-two waist and a size ten shoe. She ate junk food every day and never gained an ounce. She went to bed with all her makeup on and woke up with a clear, unblemished complexion, just like her conscience.

Mimi came to Block 122 every night, and Friday was no exception. She and Bliss Llewellyn, a tall, rangy Texan who'd recently transferred to Duchesne, had spent the afternoon primping for the evening's festivities. Or rather, Bliss had spent the afternoon sitting by the side of the bed making complimentary noises while Mimi tried on everything in her wardrobe. They'd settled on a sexy-but-in-an-off-beat-bohemian-way-with-

straps-just-falling-off-the-shoulder-just-so-Marni camisole, a tiny denim Earnest Sewn miniskirt, and a sparkly
Rick Owens cashmere wrap. Mimi liked to travel with an
entourage, and in Bliss she'd found a suitable compan-
ion. She'd befriended Bliss solely at her father's request,
since Senator Llewellyn was an important colleague. At
first Mimi had chafed at the directive, but she changed
her mind when she realized Bliss's equine good looks
complemented and emphasized her own ethereal beauty.
Mimi loved nothing more than a suitable backdrop.
Leaning against the stuffed cushions, she glanced at Bliss
approvingly.

"Cheers," Bliss said, clinking her glass against Mimi's,
as if she'd read her mind.

"To us." Mimi nodded, chugging the last of her lumi-
nescent purple cocktail. It was her fifth of the evening,
and yet she felt as sober as when she'd ordered the first
one. It was depressing how much longer it took to get
drunk now. Almost as if alcohol didn't have any effect on
her bloodstream. The Committee had told her it would
happen—she just hadn't wanted to believe it back then.
Especially since she wasn't supposed to avail herself of
the other, more potent alternative as often as she'd have
liked. The Committee had too many rules. At this point
they were practically running her life. She impatiently

signaled to the waitress to bring another round, snapping her fingers so hard it almost shattered the glass coffee table in front of her.

What was the point of going out in New York if you couldn't even get a little buzzed? She stretched out her legs and lay them languidly across the couch, her feet resting on her twin brother's lap. Her date, the nineteen-year-old heir to a pharmaceutical fortune and a current investor in the nightclub, pretended not to notice. Although it would be hard to say if he was even conscious, as he was currently leaning on Mimi's shoulder and drooling.

"Quit it," Benjamin Force snapped, brusquely pushing her off. The two of them shared the same pale, platinum blond hair, the same creamy, translucent skin, the same hooded green eyes, and the same long, slender limbs. But they couldn't have been more different in temperament. Mimi was loquacious and playful, while Benjamin—nicknamed Blackjack in childhood because of his tantrums, and shortened to Jack in adolescence—was taciturn and observant.

Mimi and Jack were the only children of Charles Force, the sixty-year-old, steely-haired media magnate who owned an upstart television network, a cable news channel, a popular newspaper tabloid, several radio stations, and a successful publishing empire that made profits from autobiographies of World Wrestling Federation stars. His wife, the former Trinity Burden, was a doyenne of the New York society circuit, and chaired the most prestigious charity committees. She was instrumental in the foundation of The Committee, of which Jack and Mimi were junior members. The Forces lived in one of the most sought-after addresses in the city, a luxurious, well-appointed townhouse that covered an entire block across from the Metropolitan Museum of Art.

"Oh c'mon," Mimi pouted, immediately placing her feet back on her brother's lap. "I need to stretch my legs. They're so sore. Feel," she demanded, grabbing a sinewy calf and asking him to feel the muscle tense underneath. Strip Cardio was a bitch on the joints.

Jack frowned. "I said quit it," he murmured in his serious voice, and Mimi immediately retracted her tanned legs, tucking them beneath her butt and letting the undersoles of her four-inch Alaïa heels scrape against the white suede couch, leaving dirty scratch marks on the immaculate cushion.

"What's wrong with you?" Mimi asked. Her brother had arrived in a foul mood just a minute ago. "Thirsty?" she taunted. Her brother was such a party pooper lately. He hardly ever went to Committee meetings anymore, something their parents would freak out about if they ever found out. He wasn't dating anyone; he looked weak and spent, and he was undeniably cranky. Mimi wondered when the last time was that he had had any.

Jack shrugged and stood up. "I'm going out to get some air."

"Good idea," Bliss added, rising in a hurry. "I need a smoke," she explained apologetically, waving a pack of cigarettes in front of Mimi's face.

"Me too," Aggie Carondolet, another girl from Duchesne said. She was part of Mimi's crowd, and looked just like their leader, down to the five-hundred-dollar highlights and sullen expression.

"You don't need my permission," Mimi replied in a bored voice, although the opposite was true. One didn't simply leave Mimi's presence—one was dismissed.

Aggie smirked, and Bliss smiled nervously, following Jack toward the back of the club.

Mimi shrugged. She never bothered to follow the rules, and tended to light up wherever and whenever she felt like it—the gossip columns once gleefully published the five-figure tally of her smoking fines. She watched the three of them leave, disappearing into the crush of bodies throwing themselves around the dance floor to obscene rap lyrics.

"I'm bored," she whined, finally paying attention to the guy who had hardly left her side all evening. They had been dating for all of two weeks, an eternity on the Mimi time line. "Make something happen."

"What do you have in mind?" he murmured groggily, licking her ear.

"Mmmm," she giggled, putting a hand underneath his chin and feeling his veins throb. Tempting. But maybe later, not here, not in public at least. Especially since she'd just had her fill of him yesterday . . . and it was against the rules . . . Human familiars were *not* to be abused, blah, blah, blah. They needed at least a forty-eight-hour recovery time . . . But oh, he smelled wonderful . . . a hint of Armani aftershave . . . and underneath . . . meaty and vital . . . and if she could just get one little taste . . . one little . . . bite . . . but The Committee met downstairs, right beneath Block 122. There could be several Wardens here, right now . . . watching . . . She could be caught. But would she? It was dark in the VIP room . . . Who would even notice in this crowd of self-involved narcissists?

But they would find out. Someone would tell them. It was eerie how they knew so much about you—almost as if they were always there, watching, inside your head. So, maybe next time. She would let him recuperate from last night. She ruffled his hair. He was so cute—handsome and vulnerable, just the way she liked them. But for now, completely useless. "Excuse me for a second," she told him.

Mimi leaped from her seat so quickly that the cocktail waitress bringing a tray of lychee martinis to the table did a double take. The crew around the banquette blinked. They could have sworn she was sitting down just a second ago. Then in a flash, there she was: in the middle of the room, dancing with another boy—because for Mimi, there was always another boy, and then another and another, each one of them all too happy to dance with her—and it seemed like she danced for hours—her feet never even touching the ground—a dizzying, blond tornado in eight-hundred-dollar heels.

When she came back to the table, her face glowing with a transcendental light (or merely the effects of bene-*f*it high beam?), her beauty almost too painful to bear—she found her date sleeping, slumped over the edge of the table. A pity.

Mimi picked up her cell phone. She just realized that Bliss had never returned from that cigarette break.